I0555527

SAKAYO

A Novel

Saa Maurice Sindondoeh Jumu

Sierra Leonean Writers Series

SAKAYO

ISBN: 978-9988-8743-5-3

Sierra Leonean Writers Series
Warima/Freetown/Accra
120 Kissy Road, Freetown, Sierra Leone
Kofi Annan Avenue, North Legon, Accra, Ghana
Publisher: Prof. Osman Sankoh (Mallam O.)
publisher@sl-writers-series.org
www.sl-writers-series.org

Dedication

This book is dedicated to the following:
My wife, Halima Sedia Jumu (Lecturer, Milton Margai College of Education and Technology),
My children; Betty, Kasay, Tambay and Hannah Holima
My grand children, Jamestina and Halima Sesay
The entire Jumu family

Acknowledgments

My sincere thanks go to the following people:

My late mother, Sia Hawa Jumu, popularly known as Koboeh, for her storytelling lessons that kept the fire burning in me to write my own stories.

The entire farming community in Kambaya, for the animated storytelling sessions which was organized for the neighborhood children, including me.

My late uncle, Komba Jumu, nicknamed Okonkwo, a retired Military Serviceman, who helped laid my educational foundation.

Mr. Alan Davison, for making literature very interesting to me at Jaiama Secondary School

Mr. D. H. Wilkes, for encouraging me to read many novels

Haja kadie Kamara and Bai Tejan Kargbo for typing the Manuscripts

Messers Komba David Sandi, Harry O. T. Lebbie and Emmanuel Senessie for editing the Manuscripts

My special thanks to my Publisher Prof Osman Sankoh (Mallam O of SLWS) and his staff.

Chapter One

At the Break of the School Day

The school bell rang and the children shouted ay-ay-ay. It was exactly 2 pm at Kayima Methodist Primary School, and time to go home. As soon as the teachers stepped out of the classrooms, the children rushed out to the football pitch which was about ten meters away from the four identical school buildings. They chased each other on the pitch whilst some played football. But there was one group that walked across the pitch to the main road that went to the towns and villages south of Kayima. They had to walk between four and six kilometers and they were hungry. That was why they had no time to play but to go quickly through the distance ahead of them. They were determined to arrive home in good time, eat any food that was available in the town or village or follow their parents to their farms. Their parents most often ensured that food was made available in the farms so that in the evening the children may fetch enough fire wood for cooking that may last for some days. As they went across the football pitch that day, they wondered where would find food, at home or in the farm? They increased their pace to get to the nearest town. Aiah Tomossi and his sister Yei led the group of boys and girls that afternoon. They were far ahead of the others because they were going to Siwaya which was the farthest village. If they did not walk fast enough they would arrive in the village late and may not be able to go to the farms. And if it happened that on that day their share of food was in the farm, it meant that they would stay on empty stomach until the return of their parents from the farms in the

1

evening. That was why they walked so fast, it was as if they were running.

The pupils who played on the football pitch were from Kayima town which was about four hundred meters away from the School. They stayed and played all sorts of games until they became tired and hungry and the latter forced them to go home. They took their school bags or books and walked in small groups and before they knew it they were already on top of the hill over-looking Kayima Town.

It was indeed a beautiful and a well planned Town with the houses built in straight lines with a lot of space in between them. The streets run parallel to the main motor road which passed through it, almost dividing it into two equal parts. On the right hand side of the hill was a thick forest of mango trees which were planted there by community laborers for the benefit of the Colonial District Commissioner. But when the British rule ended, the property reverted to the community with the chief as caretaker. The mangoes then became available to the community members, especially the children who love mangoes so much. In the months of May and June the flowers on the mangoes transformed themselves into ripe fruits which caught the eyes of the children as they walked past the trees every day, either on their way to school, their gardens, or farms. Not all of them had good skills to climb the trees which were big and tall. To harvest the fruits some of them made piles of stones which they hurled at the fruits one after another to dislodge as many fruits as they could. Sometimes this method paid off but it took a lot of effort and most often it did not offer them the best mangoes. Climbing the trees was the best option. It was risky and dangerous and many children avoided it on the advice of their parents. But despite the advice some still climbed without incidence while others fell off sustaining minor injuries which they hid as long as it was not on their faces. Others had serious injuries which cost their parents lots of money in hospital bills.

Sakayo was one of pupils that climbed a tree one afternoon with Kaye on the ground to gather whatever he was able to drop down. It was indeed a difficult climb because he chose a big tree which had a lot of ripe mangoes. Fortunately, he was skilful enough to overcome all the obstacles that he faced. After some time he reached the branch with ripe mangoes. "Kaye watch out", he said as he began dropping some mangoes to the ground. He continued dropping the mangoes until his hands could no longer reach the ripe ones. He went up higher and walked on a branch to the extreme edge holding firmly unto another branch over his head. It was indeed a dangerous venture as he bounced up and down as if he was on a see-saw. He was desperate for the mangoes and he got them. Kaye kept moving from one point to another picking up the mangoes and heaping them in a single pile. He had no machete so he used his bare hands to pull apart thorns when they crossed his path or to tear away leaves that hide any fallen mangoes. He made sure he did not lose any despite the thick bush surrounding the trees.

When Sakayo realized he could no longer reach the mangoes, he shook the branches vigorously, a process which scattered both ripe and green mangoes far and wide from the base of the tree, making Kaye's work much more difficult but not beyond his ability. He increased his speed and moved about quickly picking mangoes that were not severely damaged from the impart of their fall. When he was quite convinced he had dropped enough mangoes he descended the tree and made two piles of the mangoes and selected the one closer to him. He removed his books from his bag and put the mangoes in it.

Kaye was not satisfied because he had more green mangoes in his pile. He felt that Sakayo was not fair with him and argued on the method of sharing. The argument almost turned into a fight when they came very close to Mr. Mani Nyama's home. Mani was initially a rice farmer but later became a diamond Mining License Holder. He received as support a bag of rice monthly, shovels and assorted digging tools and gravel washing sieves. The supporter got 70% of the profit after expenses whilst Mani got 30%. Whenever he found diamonds the supporter's expenditure for the operations shot up and there was no way he could deny it because he did not keep any records. That affected his earnings for the time he was a miner. When he came back to Kayima, he was well off compared to the farmers but going forward he could not keep his riches due to inappropriate planning and domestic problems. As for his supporters, he learnt that they were big businessmen in Freetown and in The Gambia. Mani later worked in many towns and villages where diamond mining was practiced with good results but he was not fortunate enough to find as much money as he had on previous occasions. It was at that point in time that he returned home and fell back on rice farming as a last resort. In that period he had a series of broken marriages due to the change in his financial status leaving him a single parent with many children who were barely managing to go to school with support from his rice and cassava farms. Mani loved his children and supported their education fully because he believed that if he was educated he could have kept records of the supporter's expenditure and his share of funds would have been far bigger than what he got out of their mining operations. He loved other children as well and paid attention to them, especially when they were in trouble. One day he came across a group of pupils who had surrounded one of their schoolmates when school was out. He dashed there quickly and found that one pupil had struck another in the eye accidentally whilst they were playing. He stopped a taxi and took the boy to the Koidu government hospital and informed his parents immediately. The injury was serious but the timely intervention of a doctor saved the eye. From that experience Mani made it a habit to watch and listen to children whenever they gathered together to play. He saved many children from danger or from acting on some wrong decisions that could have resulted into some mishap. That was the main reason why he invited the two boys that quarreled close to his house into his verandah. When the two walked in, they were tense and their countenances showed anger. "I am quite sure that your parents have told you not to fight but to complain to your teachers or to any elder. You have ignored your parents' advice because you are almost about to fight without making any complaints anywhere. Now tell me who you are and what has happened that has made you so bitter against each other", he asked pointing at the one that had already removed his uniform and was prepared for a fight.

"My name Is Kaye, both of us picked mangoes which he shared, making sure that I had green ones for which I am not satisfied", he explained. "What is your name and tell me how you shared the mangoes?" asked Mani. "My name is Sakayo. I made two piles of the mangoes and selected the one close to me. He was not happy and said that I did not have enough food at home that was why I took the best Mangoes" he said. "Where and how did you pick the mangoes?" Mani asked Kaye again. "We picked the mangoes at the former residence of the District commissioner. Sakayo climbed the tree and I gathered whatever he dropped on the ground", Kaye explained. "Now listen to me, I am going to share these mangoes fairly, taking into account the information that you have provided. Please put all of them on the table close to the door and see what I will do", he instructed. They obeyed and put all the mangoes on the table into two separate groups. He went to the table and mixed them up completely so that each one lost its identity in the big group.

"Now, I am ready to share the mangoes. Sakayo, you are number one and Kaye number two. When I call out your number, please go to the table and select any mango that pleases you. Do you understand me, he asked them? Ok if you do, Sakayo please tell me what your number is?" he asked. "Number one" he said. "What about you Kaye?" he asked

"Number two" He said. He held his breath for a few seconds and then shouted "Number one" and Sakayo went to the table and took one ripe mango. "Number two" and Kaye went over and took one ripe mango. And it continued in that manner until all the fourteen mangoes were selected. Each of the boys looked at his share and smiled. "If both of you are satisfied, shake hands," requested Mr. Mani. The boys shook hands and burst into laughter.

They said thanks and walked away to their homes. And from that day Sakayo and Kaye became intimate friends. They went to school together and returned home together. They shared their food in school. Most often Kaye brought some pan cakes and occasionally Sakayo brought mangoes and some wild edible fruits. When they played football, they were almost always in the same team. If Sakayo was the one selecting the team, he would select Kaye first before anyone else and vice versa.

Kaye stayed with his aunt Bondu who lived in Kayima Old Town, a small settlement about 200 meters away from Kayima. This town did not grow much but it gave birth to Kayima.

Bondu's husband died at a very early age, leaving her with no children. Without much support from relatives she consoled herself with the only house which they had and a piece of land with coffee plantations. She worked hard on the plantations to eke out her living, Kaye being her only helper. One day her husband's brothers laid claims on the property on a strong belief that since she had no children for her husband, she had no right to inherit the property. The dispute brought a sharp division in the family and after a series of confrontations, the matter went to court. Following a series of adjournments the verdict declared her the rightful owner of the property. From that time she lived happily in her home with Kaye.

Kaye was happy staying with his Aunt who happened to be frank and helpful. She made sure that he had enough food to eat but ensured that he too did all the chores that a young boy was expected to do. She allowed him some time to visit his friends and vice versa, making sure that they did not over stay and over play.

Chapter Two

Betty's Departure

Sakayo was fair in complexion and so thin that his clothes always appeared to be oversized. His apparently long hands floated freely in his shirt sleeves. He was so light on the ground that his friends always feared that the slightest wind would blow him over. He was barely seven years old when his father, Entona Kebbie called him into his bedroom one evening and said, "This is Aunty Nema. From now on she will take care of you". As he spoke he was standing close to the strange woman who sat on one of the chairs in the room. As far as Sakayo was concerned she was strange and to the best of his knowledge she had never been to the house before. He could still recall that Aunty Nema looked at him for a long time and he wondered why she looked at him in that queer manner. At that same moment Aunty Nema was thinking the little boy appeared to be smart and had a potential of uniting his parents in the future. That would mean she, Nema, would go without a husband. Or, at best, share Entona with another woman. But she was not too moved by what she felt at that moment because she believed what Sokiti did for her. Finally, she shook his hands firmly and gave him a broad smile despite what she felt about him at that time. The strange woman was going to take care of him, what about his mother? Was she not able to take care of him? All of these tormenting questions which he could not answer made him sick and worried. Two days before meeting Nema his mother, Betty had not returned home. She had made some cakes for him that morning and went away promising to return in the evening. Unfortunately she did not return home, deceiving her own son. Nevertheless, she cherished Sakayo but he was too young to know that his father was maltreating her and planning to marry another woman, the reason why she was abandoning the house. She knew quite well that Sakayo would not have the best of times with a step mother but she was confident that he would grow up to remember her as a caring and loving mother. She wept each time she recalled the day she gave him some sweet cakes and said she was going away to a nearby town and promised to be back in the evening. She knew she was lying and leaving him alone with no guaranties of any proper care, but it was time for her to take a firm decision about what was going on wrong in her life. She only hoped Entona's new wife would be kind to him. She left Kayima and settled in Kasay-Chaindedu with her uncle. She did not have enough money to engage in any productive business so she decided to work on her uncle's rice farm. She cooked for the organized team of farmers that came to work at intervals, weeded the farm and assisted in many other duties on the farm, including scaring weaver birds which was tasking. She was on the farm for nearly five consecutive farming years. Being young and attractive, suitors did come but she decided she was still married to Entona and until there was an appropriate divorce decision she would not condone any other relationship and she kept to that decision.

One day she did a self assessment of herself and realized that she could be a teacher. That very day she wrote an application letter to the only Primary School in the town, with Mr Moripeh as Head teacher. She just gave it a trial and was not quite sure anybody would talk to her on the same issue again. Surprisingly though it happened. She was invited to an interview a week later and she was recruited to teach in the nursery section of the school. She found the work interesting and challenging but she coped with it. Unfortunately, her services were terminated at the end of the academic year because she was unqualified and untrained. Nevertheless, she was encouraged to reapply and during the filing process she had to part with some money for her to be reengaged. At work she took three different in- service training courses which transformed her into an effective teacher. Two years later she opted for the Basic Examination certificate Examination under a Junior Secondary School in Koidu town and she was permitted to go ahead with it. She bought and read past examination questions by way of preparation. Later, she took the examinations and passed with flying colors. It was based on her successful examination results that the School's Authorities increased her salary. It was then she remembered that Sakayo needed some financial assistance. Once in a while, she would send some money to him through Biango. She never received any confirmation that Sakayo received the monies. As time went by Betty decided to prepare herself for the West African Senior Secondary School Examinations (WASSSCE) which required a lot of money and reading materials. She made contacts with friends in Koidu town and got a reasonable number of relevant books on some key subjects and she took lessons from two teachers who were appropriately qualified to teach WASSSCE examinations. While she was preparing for the examinations, Betty learnt that the Missionary who had taken her son to the Jaiama Secondary School had flown with him to the United States of America. That piece of information added to her joy and motivated her to pursue with zeal the WASSSCE examinations. Without much teaching compared to students at a normal school, Betty decided to take three subjects at a time. One day when she was in Koidu town in search of additional reading materials, she bought a mobile telephone and sent her number to the Principal of Jaiama Secondary School, with the hope that whenever Sakayo contacted them, they would give it to him. One evening when she was resting in her bedroom she got a call and surprisingly it was from Sakayo but the line broke to the extent that she did not understand clearly some of the messages, but she was very happy that he was doing very well in school.

Betty came in contact with Entona when she went to attend Yengema Secondary School. She stayed with her uncle Kai Monneh who worked for Yarya Mining Company. He lived in a section of the town referred to as Clerks Quarters. His close departmental neighbor was Entona Kebbie, a clerk in the Stores department, who was a likeable person and well known both at the work place and outside it. He was tall with thick black hair and a set of white teeth which he displayed most often because he was fond of smiling whenever he had an encounter with people. He had a sound Secondary School Education, based on which he got the job as a clerk in the company. Entona and Kai became friends and maintained an open door policy towards each other. The policy allowed the children too to move in and out of the two homes freely and at any time. Betty was barely sixteen years old then and preparing for the Basic Elementary Certificate of Education (BECE) at the Yengema Secondary School. She was tall and thin with big breasts that filled her chest completely, making her look much older than her age. She was attractive and soft spoken. At Clerks Quarters she was considered to be the most humble and best behaved girl. She was one of several children staying with Kai and she laundered and ironed his clothes and cooked whenever his wife was not available, as she was busy doing some rice farming in her village in a bid to supplement the food at home.

Entona and Betty became good friends. Their friendship was based on a give and take relationship; Entona was a bachelor and required somebody to launder his clothes for which service he was ready to pay. Betty took the job because the money could come in handy to buy lunch at school. Entona was very pleased with her commitment and thoroughness but, above all, he was fond of her. So he made frequent calls on her whenever he returned home from work. On some such occasions she found there were no clothes to laundry rather, he wanted her to answer questions relating to her parents or brothers and sisters. After some time in the job, which was a secret arrangement between them, Betty realized Entona fallen deeply in love with her and was finding an opportunity to voice it out. As a result she decided to avoid him as much as possible especially when he called at odd hours. Sometimes she would pretend to be asleep or send a false message that she had been by her uncle to buy some items in the nearby shop. But Entona was not moved by such excuses at all. He continued to provide money for lunch and biscuits whether she laundered or not and she never refused the offers. One day he left the clothes he wanted laundered in his bedroom and asked Betty to collect them but she saw the trap. So she went with a friend to remove the dirty clothes and took them to the tap where she normally laundered them. He watched the drama with amazement then became aware she was aware of his intentions. Yet he was determined not to give up and planned new strategies to get her to be alone with him in his house but without success.

Kai had no idea what was going on as Betty had made no report about any wrong doing. What he did know was that she laundered for him and in return gave her money in recognition of her helpfulness. That much he knew and he did not entertain any fears that the relationship would extend beyond that point, considering that she was under aged and attending school.

It was Easter Holidays and all schools closed down to observe it. Betty had an assignment to go home to her parents to collect some rice for the family. Kai gave her the money and all the logistics she needed to pay for the trip and decided on the date of departure. A day before she left Yengema, she informed Entona that she would be away for at least a week, but she would identify another person to launder for him while she was away. Entona then gave her some money and promised to see her in her village but Betty thought it was joke and didn't take him seriously.

At work the next day Entona applied for Casual Leave to attend to an urgent family matter but he did not get an immediate approval as he had work at hand in the office. However, the next day he saw his manager and made a passionate appeal for him to approve his Leave because Entona was a good worker at work his application was reconsidered and by the end of the day, it was approved. The next morning he went to the bank and withdrew a reasonable sum of money for a trip to Tefeya the town close to Betty's village. He bought three cartons of assorted soft drinks and some quantities of Star beer,

Stout and some food stuff. When he acquired all that he needed for the journey, he boarded a taxi cab to the village, which was on the Highway to Kayima if one took the road which led to Yormadu town. Within an hour and half he arrived in Sengekor by which time the waning sunlight was hiding behind the tall trees surrounding the village. A cool breeze was blowing which kept the villagers cool and refreshed. Entona appreciated the weather which was a complete opposite of what he had left around Yengema

When he arrived in Sengekor, he looked around and saw a young man in whom he asked for his lodgings. The young man agreed to put him up. He left his luggage with the driver and climbed onto the verandah where he sat in a hammock. "My name is Entona and I am happy to be your guest tonight" and shook his hand vigorously. "My name is Fengo Duti, and you are welcome to my house", the youth replied following him to the car to collect luggage. Along the way the two got into a lively discussion during which they got to know more about each other. They took out the drinks and luggage from the car and took them to an inner room where he had lodged Entona.

After dinner the two men sat conversing on the verandah. As they conversed they shared their experiences at which time Entona explained why he was in Sengekor. "I am on leave at my work place but I am here to locate a girl I love and would like to marry. It is kept between the two of us and none of her relatives has known my intention. She lives in Tefeya and she is called Betty. She is a student presently at Yengema Secondary School. I even wonder whether she is fully aware of my actual intentions. I have come to sit down with her and agree on many important issues, and I am very happy that I have found such a nice person like you. What I actual need against tomorrow is somebody to link me with her without bringing her parents into the picture" he said and stopped abruptly to hear from his host. Fengo's lips stretched backwards into a broad smile. "You are indeed a lucky fellow, first of all to lodge in my house, secondly to have me as a contact person. But, and most importantly to be here today when we have a ball dance tomorrow which has attracted the youths in every village or town in our community including youths from Tefeya. I know the girl in question very well and her parents know me too. Two years ago I participated fully in the celebrations leading to her initiation in the Bondo Society. As long as marriage is your main objective, you will have support from many relatives and friends including me. As for the contact, I will be in her house first thing in the morning" he assured him. "Thank you very much. I feel at home with you. Please let us entertain ourselves" Entona suggested and brought out the crates of beer and stout. They drank until late at night when they parted company.

Very early the next morning Fengo came to him to say that he was ready for the trip to Tefeya in line with his initial request to contact Betty. He came out of the room, greeted him and gave him some money for the trip. "It is a walking distance and I have decided to walk as a form of exercise" Fengo said trying to refuse the money. But Entona insisted "Take the money because you need it. You told me that there will be a ball dance here tonight; don't you think you may need it out there? And if I may ask, what is the cost of a ticket to the dance?" He asked

"It is ten thousand Leones ($1.3) per head and the organizers have put them on sale since yesterday" he said. "Do you think it will be a good idea if we bought five tickets for Betty and her friends?" he asked, convinced that Fengo would endorse it. "Yes, it is a wonderful idea. It leaves Betty no tangible excuse but to come for the dance. However, my concern is the number of tickets. In case she does not have as many as four friends, which will be a waste of money. Do you see my point?" He asked. "You are correct but she can make new friends with the tickets. I don't have any problems with the payment" he assured him. Entona put his hand into his pocket and brought out fifty thousand Leones ($6.7) and gave to him. Fengo received the money and wondered whether his guest wasn't a rich man as he did not mind spending money on people he did not know. He went back into the town and bought five tickets. As he walked away towards Sengekor, his mind focused on Betty's family with a suitor working for a big company. He regretted that his daughter Sia did not go to secondary school to be able to attract a good suitor like Entona. She dropped out at primary school due to pregnancy barely one year after spending a lot of money to get her initiated in the Bondo Society. The teacher she claimed was responsible for the pregnancy was contacted but he denied the accusation and within days he was transferred to a school in Koidu town. He must have spent a reasonable amount of money to get his transfer done quickly to escape the scene. The matter died a natural death because Fengo did have enough money to pursue it. He was required to make a report at the police station in Kayima. A police officer was to be assigned to the case and to arrest the accused person in Koidu Town. All transportation costs involved were to borne by Fengo. What more, the case was to be referred to Police Headquarters at Motema, where he was required to take the victim after obtaining a medical report from the hospital which he had to produce at the police station. And whenever the case was charged to court, he was required to consult a lawyer whose fee would be as high as the annual income of an average rice farmer. Although radio programs have taught them that there were free lawyers for such matters, they were found mostly in the cities and to contact them meant money. The array of expenditure involved to seek redress was too much for a rice farmer. That was why he took care of his daughter until she gave birth to a baby girl, although it meant additional responsibility for him. It was an agonizing task which negatively his social statuses in his town; especially when Sia's friends visited her in school uniform while she nursed her baby. Those were embarrassing moments not only for Sia, but for him as her father. If, on the other hand she returned to school, it would be in another town far away from Sengekor. But even there, it would require a lot of money which he did not have at that moment. Fengo was so lost in his thoughts he was surprised when he realized he was already in Tefeya. He went straight to Betty's house. He was happy because he found her alone at the back of the house. It was indeed an embarrassing moment not only for her but for him as the father. If she should go to school again, it would be in another town far away from Sengekor and that would also require a lot of money which was not available at that moment. He was completely lost in his thoughts until he realized suddenly that he was already in Tefeya. He went straight for Betty's house. He was happy because he found her alone at the

17

back of the house. "Where are your parents?" he asked to know exactly where they were. "They went to the farm to harvest some yams for me" she said and continued sweeping around the house. "Do you know a man by the name Entona?" he asked. She stopped sweeping abruptly and concentrated on him for more information. "Yes I know him. What has happened to him?" She asked, curious to get to the bottom of the matter quickly. "He is quite well and as I speak to you, he is staying in my house and he is on Leave" he explained having seen anxiety on her face. But then surprisingly, her facial expression became sad and she went into deep thoughts, staring at him but without winking her eyes. "I am sorry if I said anything that has affected you. I am not lying to you. He is with me and if you doubt it please come along with me" He emphasized to her. "He is a good man". She replied. "One day he told me that he will come to my village but I thought it was a joke. I am sorry I was trying to assess why he came here in the first place. Anyway, he is your guest and not mine, so please take good care of him" She explained, in an effort to put him at ease. "By the way, are you coming to the dance tonight? I have in my possession five tickets; one for you and four for your close friends. He produced the tickets and handed them to her. Entona bought these tickets and he hopes to see you and your friends tonight" He concluded and waited for her final reaction. She looked at the ticket curiously and then shook her head before she spoke out. "I had decided not to attend the ball dance but now I am constrained by the tickets. Anyway, tell him that I will be there with my friends" She concluded and moved around the house to collect the dirt mostly composed of dried leaves. Fengo got up in a happy mood and returned to Sengekor.

Entona waited and became impatient. He came out of his room and walked along the road to Tefeya. He walked a long distance without knowing it. Then he saw Fengo. "My friend your absence was like two days to me. Thank God you are back safe and sound. Please give me a good story to justify your long stay" Said Entona, hoping to hear some good news. "She is coming with her friends. But for the tickets, she was not prepared to attend the dance. You are indeed a smart guy" Said Fengo smiling. Entona rushed at him and shook his hand vigorously. He took one hundred thousand Leones from his pocket, handed it to him and whispered into his ear. "This sum of money is for you and whosoever you may wish to invite to the dance" He said smiling. "Thank you very much. Nobody has been so generous to give me such a huge sum of money. I will explain to my children this exceptional gift from you" He said putting the money deep into his pocket. They two men returned home and continued drinking while getting ready for the dance. Late in the afternoon, the Amplifier Set, mounted on a vehicle cruised into town blasting reggae music from big speakers, sending music across the town to the nearby towns and villages. Within a short time youths across the region came into the town in small groups until the area around the youth centre became full. Ticket sales were at an advance stage and the dance looked promising. The youth centre, the Dance Hall opened immediately when the organizers where satisfied with the sales and the dance began in earnest.

Betty and her friends arrived at Sengekor and went to Fengo's house before continuing to the dance. It all looked good with Entona and Betty at the rear and Fengo leading the way with the other girls following his footsteps sheepishly, as if he was pulling them along on a rope. A few minutes' walk brought them to the Youth Centre, into the thick of the music. They presented their tickets at the gate and they were immediately allowed into the Hall. It was all joy as the music changed from one piece to another and the youths danced themselves out. It continued like that with no breaks as the generator fed the current into all the appliances to sustain the music at a high pitch. After hours of continuous dancing, Entona asked Fengo and the girls to go with to his lodge for some refreshment. They agreed and went along with him to Fengo's house, where he had kept the assorted drinks in a cooler. A table was set and the service began immediately. Coca-Cola, Fanta, maltina, sprite, star beer and stout were the drinks available. They girls chose soft drinks whilst the two men, as usual chose Star beer and Stout. Entona served Coca-cola, Fanta, and Sprite to Betty's friends and reserved Maltina for Betty. They drank three bottles each over a period of nearly an hour. When they were satisfied, Betty's friends indicated that they would like to return to the dance. "Good, said Entona. Fengo please go with them and I and Betty will join you within the next fifteen minutes" he said confidently.

Fengo led the girls to the dance and stayed with them. Meanwhile Entona discussed lengthily his intention to marry Betty whilst they were alone but she appeared to be weak after drinking the last bottle maltina. She initially attributed her weakness to the vigorous manner she danced to a particular piece of music she loved much. She went outside the house and washed her face with cold water but she did not get better. Eventually she fought but could not resist what appeared to be a deep sleep. Then Entona locked the doors and windows and jumped on her. She knew what was happening to her but she was too weak to resist. Of course, she shouted but the house was empty and the blast of the music across the town drowned out her tiny voice. She came to herself about midnight and when she assessed what had happened to her, she wept bitterly and refused to be consoled. Entona kept assuring her that everything would be Ok. She dressed up and went to the Youth Centre where she found her friends, tired and ready to go home. Within a short time some other boys from Tefeya joined them for the return journey. With the help of bright searchlights they made their way quickly to Sengekor as Motorbikes were not available at that time of the night. Betty did not explain to her friends what transpired between her and Entona but it occupied her mind fully. That night she did not have much sleep. She lay in bed and tried to think where she went wrong to have been an easy victim. She could not understand why she became weak suddenly after she drank the maltina which Entona offered her. Could it be the case that he put some drugs into the drink to make her weak? She realized too that she was the only one who had the Maltina drinks. She had already secretly asked her friends how they felt after the service, and they confirmed that it was refreshing. This convinced her that the only thing that made her weak and drowsy was some drug put purposely in her drink. She realized too the number of tickets bought was a bait to ensure that she went to the dance so that he could use his drugs to achieve his goal. When she came to that point she wept in her heart but only sobbed quietly so as not to create any alarm at home. The next day she put together all the food items that her parents had gathered and the day after cut short her stay and left for Yengema.

Entona woke up the next morning feeling guilty about what he did to Betty but promised in his heart that he would do everything possible to marry her. He had fried plantains for breakfast, after which he joined Fengo to find out what he felt about the dance and he told him that it was excellent. Entona was happy that he did not comment on why he and Betty never showed up again in the dance after the refreshment. He went into the bedroom and packed his belongings neatly into his suitcase. He left Fengo the remaining drinks, food items, and some money. He also provided him his contact numbers and address. Finally he was ready for his return trip. The moment a taxi To Yengema was available, he boarded it. Within an hour and half he was already in his quarters at Yengema.

Betty returned to Yengema with a change of attitude. She became thoughtful and most often she preferred to be alone in her room pretending to be reading. But the truth of the matter was that she was still assessing what had happened to her and the consequences on her schooling. One day Entona went to see her when he learnt that Kai had gone to Koidu Town. He drew Betty aside and whispered in her ears that he had a big gift for her at home and left abruptly before the other kids took notice of him. Betty waited a few minutes and then went to his quarters. She too wanted to know why he deliberately put a drug in her drink to rape her. She fearlessly went right into his bedroom where he waited. "You are wicked to have put a drug into my drink so you can get what you wanted" she burst into tears not caring whether anybody was listening to them. At the top of voice she shouted "You will surely pay for what you have done to me" Entona became a worried man, moving in and out of the house, not knowing exactly what to do. He feared that she may cause a crowd to gather and the public may know. He opened his suitcase and brought out the sum of five hundred thousand Leones and gave it to her. She received it and threw it at him violently. "Betty, I will lose my job and go to jail if you don't stop what you are doing now" he wept openly like a child. "What do you want" asked Entona, confused. "I want nothing but the truth. Did you put some drug into my drink? I will not leave here until I know the truth and my uncle will know everything" she emphasized. Entona saw the desperation on her face and yielded before it became explosive. "I am sorry for what happened. I am guilty, please forgive me" he pleaded with tears in his eyes. The moment she noticed that he was crying she changed her tone of voice. "What plans do you have for me in case I am pregnant" she asked. "I will marry you and stand by you forever" he assured her. He looked around, located the five hundred thousand Leones and gave it to her again and requested she should see him late the next day for proper briefing of his plans for her. Later they met often in secret and their relationship became much more cordial. For a while she appeared to be normal and responded positively to any piece of assignment she was asked to do at any time. But with time she became withdrawn and most often she hid herself from the public and sat in her bedroom for most of the day. Then Kai learnt from her teachers that she missed classes in school for a week on flimsy excuses and for various illnesses. It was based on such findings that Kai sent her to hospital for a proper check- up. A pregnancy test proved her to be positive and that piece of news was not only shocking to Kai, but to the entire settlement at the Clerks quarters. A series of interviews were conducted with her to know exactly who made her pregnant. But she refused to cooperate until she was asked to leave the house if she did not show who made her pregnant. It was then that she disclosed that Entona made her pregnant. That piece of information took everybody by surprise. Kai was so much annoyed that he called the Family Support Unit of the Police immediately. Before the officer arrived, Betty had disappeared from home. A quick search in the quarters to locate her proved unsuccessful. However, Kai continued his search by contacting his friends and relatives in the neighborhood. The next day a delegation of the community elders, mobilized and influenced indirectly by Entona and led by Chief Senesie Gbabai came to see Kai in his sitting room. The children were asked outside of the room before the meeting commenced. The chief explained that they were there to make a statement concerning Betty and he then asked Entona to say what he had to say. He came forward, cleared his throat and looked around before he opened his mouth to say anything. He was timid and afraid and was not too sure whether a plain clothes policeman was not already hiding somewhere around to arrest him. Finally convinced that he was secured, he admitted openly that he made Betty pregnant and apologized to Kai for the embarrassment that he had caused to him personally and the entire community. He promised to take full responsibility for the pregnancy and assured him that she would continue her schooling again exactly six months after she had given birth. He passionately appealed that the matter be treated at the traditional level without the involvement of the police. He then revealed that he had asked her to move out of the house and hide herself in a secret location which he had arranged to avoid any police interrogations, and further revealed that she was safe where she had taken refuge. To conclude, he promised to abide by whatever was agreed in the meeting as a final solution to the matter relating to the pregnancy and the associated responsibilities. Already the community elders had been to the Family Support Unit of the Police to inform the officer in charge that they were handling the matter at the traditional level and that whatever came out of it, they would get back to them. That was probably why there was no police presence in the meeting when Entona made his confession.

Before the intervention of the elders, Kai was called upon to respond to Entona's confession. He stood up and tried to make a speech but his voice failed him. He could not get the words out because of anger. Finally, when he got some words out, they clearly explained his position in the whole matter. He wanted the police to handle the whole affair because he was determined to punish Entona for behaving recklessly to somebody he called his friend. He knew quite well that if the matter went to the courts, he would pay dearly for his careless and reckless behavior. The elders were somehow embarrassed by his statement and reacted individually:

"If the police themselves allow us to handle a matter, why are you still referring the matter to them? You must respect our views because the solution which we are going to provide would be significantly different from that of the police. In fact, ours will have a better human face" argued one elder. " I am sorry sir, please go ahead with whatever you think is the way forward to this matter", Kai said disgustedly. The elder continued "One thing that has made the matter very simple is the fact that Entona has made a very straight forward confession. If the matter went to court he might be sent to prison for a long time as a punishment for his crime. But mind you, Betty and the child would suffer without an appropriate support from him assuming that the parents do not have the means to do so. In such a case our tradition ensures that he marries Betty and supports her and her child for life. "That is a better punishment than keeping him idle in prison" said a second elder. "Kai, please accept the traditional option because it offers a solution with no losers. Mark you; we can no longer make Betty as innocent as she was before Entona met her. She is pregnant and expecting a bouncing baby. This is the reality no matter what we do now," said the third elder. The matter was hotly debated and at the end it was agreed that Entona must marry Betty within a month and must prepare himself for an abridged version of the Kono traditional marriage because the pregnancy preceded the marriage. However, the calabash required and its normal contents were expected to be a key element in the process. Kai and his relatives accepted the solution provided by elders and hoped that Entona would go according to his promises as they had not allotted any punishment to Entona if he did not go according to the promises. Should such a situation arise however, they themselves would normally provide support to the victim facing such circumstances. Entona and Betty were happy because their relationship which was hidden and criminal was now recognized and approved. It was no longer secret and so she came out of hiding and joined the others at home and interacted freely with Entona according to the instructions of the elders. His happiness was underlined by a huge responsibility which needed to be accomplished within a month. If he failed to obey the instructions of the elders, the matter might be taken up by the police whom he has tried as much as possible to avoid. Entona required some additional money to undertake the wedding and he needed to get it fast. So he met his relatives and friends and asked for their contributions towards his wedding. He got a reasonable purse out of his endeavor and prepared for the wedding which would finally put to rest the fear of being reported to the police.

The elders emphasized that the marriage would be an abridged one because the pregnancy preceded it. That meant too the ceremony itself was going to be short and without much fanfare. However, the key element in the traditional marriage, the Calabash would be there with its full complements. With that in mind, Entona rallied around some elderly women to take him through the process, by helping him to buy the items required before the stipulated date. The community elders were the first to be invited to the marriage which was to take place at Kai's home one Saturday evening. On that day relatives and friends cautiously gathered at Kai's home and waited patiently for an early commencement. There was a scourge ravaging the country and it was against the interest of the community to bring a large number of people together without the permission of Health Officers. The house was not full to capacity but it was highly representative. The occasion commenced with a traditional song which all the women sang and danced to joyfully. Food and drinks were served as the ceremony was on going. Before nightfall, the formalities were almost completed. The Calabash was presented and the contents were examined and adopted. Entona and Betty became husband and wife and the crowd cheered them as they stood up to take oaths. At the end of the year there was a bouncing baby boy named Sakayo. Entona continued working for the company until he was made redundant at the end of the fourth year after his marriage. The redundancy forced him to resettle in Kayima with his family. Everything worked well with Betty managing the home whilst Entona supported her fully in managing the home in the way possible. There was already an existing vacancy for the post of Court Chairman in Kayima with a key requirement that the holder must be somebody literate in English with some work experience. Entona applied for the post without much delay and the interview was conducted after a month. He got the job being the most experienced among the four applicants for the post. He was a very happy man when chief Soui told him he got the job. He had already decided to cultivate some annual crops like groundnuts and cocoa yams as his main preoccupation in Kayima but the new job completely changed his plans. If he did any farming, it would be because he had a passion for farming.

Chapter Three

Lahai Shows up

Many years later Fengo received a visitor in the person of Lahai Senesie who requested to see the chief of Sengekor in connection with Sia, Fengo's daughter. The Chief assembled his men without any delay to know why the young man came to see him. In a meeting with Fengo and the Chiefs, he identified himself as Lahai Senesie, a former teacher of the only primary school in the village. Many of the chiefs did not remember him but Fengo did but he was not in any haste to say anything until he knew why he was there. When the chiefs assembled he was given the opportunity to introduce himself and he gave a vivid description of certain memorable events that occurred at the time he was there. Thereafter he was remembered and identified as one that once lived with them. Then he was asked to state his case and he was bold enough to state that he was the one who made Sia, Fengo's daughter, pregnant but his posting to Koidu town and the financial requirements to set up a new home left him broke, the reason why did not show up to the parents to take responsibility for his action. He furthered that he learnt later that she got married because she waited for him for far too long but he did not show up to confront her parents on the issue. Continuing, he stated that Mariama was his daughter and he came to claim her and to make the process official and legal. The chiefs consulted briefly and appointed chief Biango to interrogate all the individuals concerned, who then asked that Sia should appear before him and she did with immediate effect. "Do you know Mr Lahai and was he the one who made you pregnant when you were a teenage girl in school?" he asked "Yes chief, he was the one. He made a duty schedule for cleaning the classroom and brushing around it. The boys took care of the brushing and the girls took care of sweeping and dusting the tables and desks. He puts me twice in a week on the schedule and the cleaning took place at the end of the school day. He initially went away but returned to find me alone cleaning the classroom. He proposed love and ensured that we made love against my will each time I was on duty. I found it difficult if not impossible to refuse him at that time and I was afraid to report him to my parents until I became pregnant" She replied. "Fengo, what action did you take to protect your daughter and the baby" asked Chief Biango. "I am sorry I did not take any action at that time because it required police investigation and ultimately court action, all of which required money and I was barely managing to feed the family with a big farm to plow against an unstable season. But I waited for an appropriate time which has never come up to this time" he explained. "Are you married, and if that is the case why did you not marry Sia?" He asked. "Sia got married earlier than me because she was tired of waiting and I don't blame her for that. Then I got married later" He explained. "How much support did you give to her and her baby?" The chief asked again. "Honestly, I have not done what was required of me and that is the more reason why I am here appealing for mercy. "So you know that you are guilty?" He asked. "Yes, I am guilty to all the parties concerned" Senesie replied. The chiefs consulted again and decided the following fines which the Chief Biango announced on the spot; "You are fined one hundred thousand Leones for creating the emergency meeting of the chiefs, one hundred thousand Leones for obstructing Sia's learning as a teenager, five hundred thousand Leones for causing obstructions in Sia's marital life, for failing to marry her at the appropriate time, and one million Leones to Fengo for his domestic expenses for sia and Mariama up to date. "Sia are you satisfied with the fines?" asked the chief. "Chief, I am happily married to Saa Tako, a decent farmer who has taken good care of me, my daughter and son. He has provided enough money to start a shop for me which is profitable enough to make us live above average. I don't need any amount from him and my daughter is not going to stay with somebody who is wicked and completely irresponsible" She explained. At the end of the meeting Lahai paid the fines. He was asked to give enough time to the chiefs to convince Sia to release Mariama, to convince her to take the surname Senessie and finally to convince her to stay with her father but Mariama refused to be separated from her mother. She continued to enjoy her step father's support until she completed school with good grades to enroll in college. Lahai kept coming but he could not convince Mariama that he was a responsible father and the matter remained an open ended affair with room for further negotiations.

Chapter Four

Entona and Nema in love

Aunty Nema appeared to be of the same age with Betty at the time she came to stay with Entona. She was of Entona's height with a stern face and unsteady eyes. At home she kept Sakayo busy with chores on a daily basis, the reason why he never stopped thinking about Betty his mother whose absence he was finally beginning to feel. He felt that if she was alive somebody would have seen her someday but nobody had seen her so far. However, if she was dead it would not be a secret forever, somebody would have known about it and the news would not remain with that person. At the end the news would get to the relatives and the truth would be known. So far, there was no such news about her and he was definitely not convinced that she was dead. She had relatives in Kayima but nobody spoke about her except Aunty Nema, the stranger.

"Do you know where your mother is presently? She asked, trying to find out how much Sakayo knew about his mother's whereabouts. "No Aunty, I don't know" he had said to her. "I leant that she is in Koidu Town, do you have any ideas?" She would inquire. "No, I don't", he had said again, and she discontinued the questioning because she got nowhere with him.

Nema Fakai was born in a village called Penduma but raised by Aunty Liza in Koidu town. She attended the Koidu town Methodist Girl's School. At the age of thirteen years she passed the National Primary School Certificate Examinations with good grades and she was admitted at the Koidu Secondary School. Nema was doing very well in school. She went through form one without any difficulties and maintain a position within the first best ten students. But late in the second form she fell outside the first ten because she started to be conscious of her beauty and joined a group of girls who felt the same way as she. All of them concentrated on make ups and idle discussions both at home and in school and the group hardly broke up. This distraction made Nema lazy and careless about the assigned pieces of work from teachers, which further caused a drop in her annual school grade. In spite of that she passed to the junior Secondary School Basic education Certificate Examination (BECE) class which was all she wanted to achieve to prove to her Aunty Liza that she was still doing well contrary to her belief that she was laggard with her school work. Nema was then barely fifteen, tall and beautiful with fluffy black hair which was most often plaited backwards into long tiny lots which fell over her shoulders, making her look even more beautiful.Close to BECE examinations, there was an annual spots Meeting for which practices were ongoing on the school's football pitch. Nema was hardly present for the practices because of her chores at home. Consequently, she was not earmarked for any particular event. But it happened that during the Meeting, the girl earmarked for the 100 meter dash from Blue House, to which Nema belonged, fell ill suddenly. The lot fell on her purely because of her height and lanky legs. She accepted the challenge. The 100 meter dash was a very important race which every spectator looked forward to. After several events, the 100 meter dash was announced and Nema ran forward from Blue House, which was not doing very well according to the records. Through the speakers the spectators heard "On your marks, get set" and a whistle sounded. As the girls took off, Nema led and sustained it through out to gain the first position. The crowd cheered her when she was pronounced the winner. Thereafter, she was positioned for all the long distance races and she did well in all of them. Her name was on every spectator's lips for her extraordinary performance and for making Blue House the winner.

Whilst members of her House were jubilating with Nema, a flashy handsome young man appeared before her, shook her hand firmly and said "You are my Queen" and then disappeared. At the end of the Meeting, she walked with a group of girls until they arrived at the junction leading to her house. As she walked along the road alone, she noticed the flashy young man followed her. That was how it appeared to her because he followed no matter which shortcut she took. Then she decided to stop to allow him to go ahead, but instead he also stopped. "Why are you following me" asked Nema "I want to have a word with you" he said boldly. "Do you realize that my house is not far away and my guardian would not like to see a boy accompanying me? Please choose another day" she said and ran away displaying her sportive quality again. She arrived home in good time and while she was alone she recalled the flashy boy. She kept wondering about who he was and what he was doing in Blue house when he was neither a teacher nor a student. She could not get to the bottom of his identity; he seemed to be a complete stranger at the sports Meeting. Yet he was desperate to speak to her in private and for that reason he was most often around her house. His behavior became worrisome to her because the number of times he showed up around the house could make

Aunty Liza become suspicious and try to find out what was happening. The flashy boy, commonly known as PK (Patrick Konga) appeared before her again when she was on her way home from school. He stretched out his hand and gave her a small box which appeared to be a mobile telephone from the image on the side of it. "This is a gift for you. Please reply my text messages and call me whenever you are alone" he said and tried to move away quickly as if somebody had spotted them. He did not even hear the thank you from her but appreciated her broad smile much. She opened the small box and saw the mobile telephone which was already with a Sim Card and fully charged. That was her first telephone and she loved it much. She put it on silent and placed it under her books in her school bag. When she was alone in her bedroom, she checked the telephone and found some messages from PK. "I have found you in good time and I will never leave you. You are my heart's desire above everything else. Although I will be in college by next academic year to read Economics, my heart will be full with you always" the message read. Nema's first reaction was to appreciate his ambition for higher education which coincided with the rumors that he was going to be enrolled in one of the universities the following academic year. Her replies were short with few words. "Your plans look good, stick to them and have a nice day" her message read. Later the format of text messages changed to that of a persistent request for a visit at his residence, with a full description of the location of his house. She ignored the initial requests but going forward he made sure the same request was in every text message that he sent. One day she decided to make a visit to find out what he was planning; perhaps he was about to go for his college arrangements and since he was not allowed to come to her house, he decided she should visit him instead. Many things ran through her mind as she contemplated on the visit. She dismissed any suggestions that he would attempt to rape her in broad day light with people moving up and down on the streets. Besides, she assessed him to be gentle and intelligent. Then she made a call to say she was on her way and followed the direction provided in the text messages. After a long walk she arrived at the house which was isolated from other buildings. It was well kept with beautiful flowers roundabout it. It looked like the home of a middle income person by its location and the way it was maintained. She was received in the sitting room which was well decorated with the photograph of an elderly man out numbering the other photographs in the room. There were modern facilities like a freezer, an amplifier set which played loud music, big fans all operated by a generator. He decided to show her around and she accepted. He took her to the kitchen, the guest rooms, pantry, and finally to the master bedroom where he asked her to sit down and again she accepted. In a split second he went to the door and closed it and then held her hand firmly and tried to draw her to the bed. She drew back her hand and rushed to the door. Unfortunately it was locked with key and the key was removed. She fought back any attempt to lay her on the bed. It was like a wrestling match with no winner in the first one hour. Then she became weak and shouted but the house was isolated from the others and loud music was still playing. Finally she gave up and accepted the consequences. At the end of the exercise she wept bitterly, knowing very well that she ignored all the pieces of advice from her parents and guardian that she must not allow men to tamper with her until she was of age. She felt like an outcast in her family, no longer with any dignity and respect. She returned home in a somber mood and Aunty Liza was sharp to notice that she was late. "We agreed that no school work should keep you until nightfall. Why are you late?" She asked rather furiously. "We had to complete a Topic in mathematics. I am sorry madam" She explained and burst into tears. "Are you crying because I asked a simple question? I don't believe that is why you are crying. Get up and prepare the lamp for the children's room" she instructed. Nema got up and cleaned the lamp and lighted it, still reflecting on her encounter with PK. She regretted and wished it never happened. The next thing she considered was if she got pregnant what would she do. For that she contacted her friends and some of them advised her to drink a lot of salt water as a preventive measure. Others advised her to drink red and yellow capsule tablets and any pregnancy would be destroyed. She drank all the recommended salt water and capsules but at the end of the month she noticed that she was not normal. She rang PK many times but he did not pick up the calls. The next time she rang, the voice message said the number was no longer in use. Then the true identity of PK came under scrutiny. "Was he really Patrick Konga? Where could one find his parents?" She wondered. She could not find answers to these questions; as a result she decided to go back to the house where they had the encounter. Luckily, she found the elderly man whose photograph she saw in the sitting room. "Good morning sir" She greeted politely. "Good morning young lady, can I help you?" he replied. "I am asking for Patrick Konga, commonly known as PK" She said. "I am sorry; I don't know anybody with that name. Anyway, I was away for three weeks, may be my wards know him" He said and walked to the back of the house and returned within a short time and said "They don't know him". Then tears filled her eyes immediately and she walked away quickly to make sure he did not take notice that she was weeping. She walked back home feeling completely frustrated. She recalled PK referring to the house as theirs but nobody seemed to know him there. She arrived home and went into her bedroom and wept. Aunty Liza noticed the unusual sound and went into her bedroom. Her voice faded into an inaudible whisper and her lips curved into a tender smile to show that she was OK. "What are you doing in bed at this time of the day?" She asked. "Nothing" She said and got up quickly and moved out of the room, trying to hide her tears. By the second month it became clear that she was pregnant and she sat down to plan what to do. The thought of having a baby for PK would be over her dead body. She was prepared to do anything to get rid of the pregnancy. Without wasting time she decided that she would abort the baby no matter how much it was going to cost her. She contacted her friends immediately for financial support and to identify somebody to abort her. Her friends provided some money and contacted a nurse well known for abortion. She located the Nurse and paid the required amount and the following Monday morning was set aside for the operation. She was advised not to eat any food or take medicines for whatever purpose. Nema got up early Monday morning and put on her school uniforms and hid some dresses in her school bag. She arrived at the address where the abortion was to be done. The nurse showed up and within a short time the baby was no more but she bled profusely. The nurse fought hard to stop it but the bleeding continued. But by midday the bleeding stopped partially and she put on her uniforms again and walked home with the help of her friends by her sides. She was very weak and pale. She arrived home and went straight to her bed. She told Liza that she was feverish and she bought some medication for fever and headache. She took the medication and got better afterwards. The next day, Aunty Liza went to check on her without knowing she was in the bathroom. She entered her room and saw thick blood on the bed sheet which she examined with great interest and then waited by the bed with a determined glint in her eyes. "There is blood on your bed sheet. Don't tell me what I already know. Speak the truth to save your life. I am waiting" she spoke furiously. Tears filled Nema's eyes and rolled down her body. She felt she needed her life above everything else as the pain and bleeding were getting worse. She braved it and explained the full story. "Did I not warn you on several occasions about this? Do you know the name of nurse who did the abortion?" She asked and the answers were "Yes" and "No" Aunty. Liza walked to a neighbor's house and she was driven back to her house in a car. She asked Nema to dress up properly and in the next few minutes the driver sped with them in the direction of the government hospital, where Nema was admitted. Her case was pretty serious and the medical doctor in charge treated her immediately. She was in the hospital for nearly a week until the bleeding stopped completely. She lost a lot of blood which made her very weak and completely pale. Liza bought the recommended drugs and she was discharged with an instruction not to do any physical work but to rest and take the drugs. She was further advised to skip the BECE which were a week away. Later Liza went to Tankoro Police Station and made a report about a man named Patrick Konga who raped Nema which resulted into pregnancy. Patrick escaped immediately after the incidence and she did an illicit abortion which nearly cost her her life. Asked why it was only now she was making a report of the incidence, she explained that Nema's life was at great risk and she felt she must see the Doctor first. The Police officer assigned to the matter took notes but the name of the nurse that did the abortion was not available at the time of reporting. The officer went after Patrick Konga and the nurse using the description available on them but found out they were on the run.

It was based on the Doctor's decision and the fact that her abortion was no longer a secret that Liza sent Nema back to Penduma for her to recuperate properly and it was proved beyond doubt that some of her own friends were propagating the news about her calamity. While she was in Penduma, she was well informed about what was happening in Koidu Town relating to what happened to her. It was at that crucial moment that she decided that she was no longer morally strong to stay with Aunty Liza for the purpose of schooling. She stayed in Penduma until she recuperated fully and regained her full strength. But any time she came across any of her books which she brought along with her, she recalled the sad incidence of the pregnancy and the illicit abortion. She wondered whether she would ever give birth to a child, considering the damage that was done to her by the nurse, according to the Doctor's report. At the same time she was coping with the stigma of the illicit abortion which did not remained in Koidu Town alone but was on the lips of young men and women in Penduma as well. She wondered who was behind it all. Finally, she made up her mind to get on with her life and ignore who said what. She went to the market in Koidu Town when schools were on to ensure that none of her colleagues saw her. She bought business items that were good for a Petty Trader as that was what she planned to become. She noticed that young men feared her for the illicit abortion which most believed would result into childlessness and any man who married her would be childless. Therefore, she concentrated on her business, moving from town to town with her wares on her head. It was a difficult task but she was prepared to do anything to make her goods available in many towns and villages. It was during one such an aggressive trading exercise that she met Entona in Kayima. He bought some items from her and spoke some encouraging words to her relating to marriage which moved her heart. From that day she made Kayima a key trading centre and Entona became a key customer. When she finally came to the conclusion that he loved her, she decided not to handle him single handedly to avoid any blunders that may cause the relationship to rupture too quickly.

In Penduma, she contacted her friend, an old woman who loved her and stayed close to her at the peak of her trials and assured her that one day her trials would be no more. It was that old woman who encouraged her to contact a soothsayer who would provide the means to get the man in question to marry her. She did not have any desire to go that far but she had absolute trust in the old woman, especially the words which she said to her: "Apart from the stigma, you know that you have a fault through what happened to you. Yes, you are still beautiful

41

and able to attract men, but once they know your condition, they may find an excuse to abandon you. What you need is some extra power which keeps the man constantly in love. Soothsayers can do that job for you, provided you are able to pay them. Think along these lines and take a positive step forward" she had advised. Finally she took the advice seriously and contacted a well known soothsayer called Sokiti Dufanna and explained to him her life history as required by him. "What do you want me to do when you have stated that the man in question loves you? Why don't you wait until he marries you at the appropriate time?" queried Sokiti "He may change his mind. I want him to marry me and stick with me for life" she emphasized. "Yes, that is possible if you are ready to part with six hundred thousand Leones" Sokiti said. "Please, please help me out. I am only a petty trader; I can afford three hundred thousand Leones only. I beg you, please consider my case" she pleaded. Sokiti thought over her request for a moment and accepted the said amount and went into his bedroom where he stayed for a long time. When he came out, sweat poured out from his body like tears running down the cheeks of a naughty child. Then he opened a small raffia bag and bought out a brownish powdered substance. He took a bit of it and put it in his mouth and swallowed it. "It is not poisonous by any means. Put some of it in his soup, and three times is more than enough. He will do whatsoever you ask him to do, and he will not abandon you for another woman" he said and bid her goodbye. Nema was quite happy about the assurance that Entona would be her husband as long as she carried out Sokiti's instructions. Her next trip was obviously to Kayima and before she set out, she prepared a delicious dish for

Entona which he appreciated and enjoyed. In fact, he made an appeal for more of such dishes and she was quite ready to prepare them. The intimacy and love between them increased day by day. At a point in time Entona asked her to come and stay with him. "Are you not married and living with your wife?" she asked jokingly. "My wife has abandoned me and our only son quite recently. She knows where I am but I don't know where she is right now" he said, and insisted that she should come and stay with him. A week later she took advantage of the invitation and moved to his premises.

Sakayo was under pressure to do his chores at home when Aunty Nema became fully established and took complete control of the home. In the morning he would fetch water from the tap for drinking, washing and for cooking. He swept the four roomed apartment and washed the dishes before going to school. Initially, he found it much difficult because he was much younger. But as he grew up, he took it up as a challenge. Before this time he was not late to school at all but lately he was and each time he was punished, especially for his untidiness. He had very little time to wash properly or iron his uniforms neatly. Growing up into teenage did not help him to champion his chores. Additionally, he had to launder his father's clothes, fetch firewood, and help with the cooking during the weekends. Outside these engagements, he had very little time for study and for his friends. The most difficult chore was to fetch firewood from the bush far away from the town. When he went alone he tended to concentrate more on his mother's absence. He missed her a lot and wanted to see her but when he went in a group, the jokes and the frank discussions with his colleagues took away most of the time he would normally use to think of her.

Sakayo was perpetually hungry. That was because his food ration had not increased proportionately with his growth. He had grown up reasonably well but his portion of food had remained the same. Most times he ate all his food and needed more but Aunty Nema would not give him. Yet in the cupboard there was most often food reserved for visitors and a big dish for Entona, half of which he normally ate, but he came home so late that he found him asleep most often. When he was hungry and needed some food and there was no way out to get some food, he decided to do many odd things. Most often he went to Kaye who enjoyed sharing his food with him. But one day he decided to visit Posua, another colleague. They played various games on the verandah until the dinner was ready. Posua left him and went to the kitchen at the back of the house and received his ration. He came with it and went into his room and locked the door after him. He spoke to him through a hole in the window. "Sakayo it is fish in Cassava Leaves, but not enough for me. Please next time", he said and commenced his dinner. Sakayo got up and walked away in shame. It was too late to try any other colleague, so he returned home hungry and bitter. "Sakayo where did you spend your evening?" asked Aunty Nema. "At Posua's", he said timidly. "You are now a big boy to be told every day that you have to clean the lamps and light them before night fall", she said pointing her finger at him. "By the way why did you go there?" she asked again. "To play games with him" He said. "Yes, to play games with him and to share his food, as if you are not having enough food at home. You glutinous boy!" she lambasted him.

The next day Sakayo was out in the field alone to fetch firewood after failing to convince some of his colleagues to accompany him. He did not like to be in the forest alone because he was afraid of chimpanzees. He entertained that fear but he had to go because Aunty Nema would not accept any excuses. He was out alone and forced to overcome all fears.

On one such day, just as he was about to cut a piece of dry wood, he saw some ripe wild fruits which he knew already. He stopped what he was doing and climbed the tree on which the fruits hung. He harvested a good quantity and sat down at the base of the tree and ate to his satisfaction. Then he loaded his pockets with them before cutting the wood. He returned home in a happy mood, with a big bundle of firewood which he dropped in the kitchen and ran into his room and hid the fruits in his school bag. "Sakayo, you are a wicked boy, you know exactly where to get good firewood but the last few bundles that you brought to this house were tiny and not quite useful. From now on I will examine what you are going to bring out as firewood. If they are not good enough you will go back into the bush and fetch another bundle no matter how late it might be", She threatened. Sakayo brought a big bundle each time he went out for firewood because he needed to satisfy Aunty Nema and save himself from going for another bundle in case she was not satisfied with the first bundle. He spent time looking for dry wood and then spent some additional time harvesting wild fruits and he got enough of them.

However, climbing different trees left him with wounds on his chest. At home he buttoned his shirt up to his neck so that Aunty Nema might not see the wounds. The wounds were a few minor cuts on his chest and arms which healed up and got re-opened when he continued climbing because a bundle of firewood lasted about four days and so he was out in the field immediately after the last bit was burnt. And once he was out there he was always tempted to climb trees the moment he found the fruits. He did well in school initially, particularly in Mathematics, but over the years his work deteriorated. His teacher came to his parents to find out why he did not do his assignments. Mr. Yaja was an old popular teacher who had been in the teaching field longer than anyone in the chiefdom and who had taught most of the prominent people who attended School in Kayima. He found only Aunty Nema at home and engaged her on the issue. "Your boy is clever but for a long time now he is either not doing his assignments or doing them wrongly. I have come to find out why," said Mr. Yaja. "This boy has his own room with a study table. He has all the recommended text books for his class. He has a nice school bag with pens and pencils. And above all, he has his food ration every day. Perhaps, you can tell me what more I must do to get him to perform in school." She explained. "How many hours does he take to study each day?" she asked. How many hours does he take to study each day? He asked in turn. "He finds food at home at the end of the school day and the rest of the day he has to himself. I am too busy to sit him down every day to get him to study. He is big enough to know what to do", she explained. "Well, I am doing my own bit in school as a teacher and as a parent you have to do your own bit for the child at home to contribute to his academic growth", Teacher Yaja said and then left completely discouraged about her attitude.

With an uninterrupted stay with Entona and without any attack from another woman, Nema felt confident that she had overcome. Her only worry was how soon she was going to bear a child for him. She was quite aware that some damage was done to her womb during the illicit abortion but did not know how serious it was with regard to her child bearing. She recalled quite clearly that the Doctor who saw her then was furious about the nurse that aborted her but did not explain to her in details what actually went wrong. She was quite aware too that without a child in the relationship, there was going to be some problems somewhere. As a result she consciously looked forward for a pregnancy and before one year she saw the signs and within a short time she was pregnant. What a joy she had! But the joy was short lived because by the end of the second month it wasted with a lot of bleeding which required an urgent medical attention and she was hospitalized for a week. It was from that moment that she saw some links between her pregnancy and the damage the doctor spoke about in the illicit abortion. Although, she stopped worrying about it but the fear of childlessness haunted her persistently because she knew what that meant in a relationship such as she had with Entona. At the end of every month after recuperation, she expected to see the signs of pregnancy but they were not available and she began to seek medical attention which was expensive but Entona was able to cope with it.

Many years later when she was not expecting it, she was pregnant. She kept it secret but the moment Entona knew about it, it was no longer a secret because his club members knew about it as well. She complied fully with the Doctor's instructions to rest and to stay away from any strenuous physical work. She rested for months and her joy was full as the pregnancy matured. However, close to the time of delivery complications set in. She was readmitted and was under constant surveillance. The doctors battled with her and at the end she gave birth to a baby girl, but she bled and became unconscious for days. She was revived and when she realized she had a baby girl, her joy was full again. Before she was discharged from hospital, the Doctor in charge spoke to Entona secretly that an initial damage to her womb, couple with the recent events, she was unlikely to bear another child except by God's intervention. Obviously, he was not happy but kept the information secret. A couple of days later the baby was named Mary in a brief naming ceremony without much fanfare because Nema had not fully recovered. Mary grew up experiencing love and care from her parents. She was alone at home and enjoyed every facility her parents could afford. When she enrolled in the United Methodist Primary School Kayima, Nema's burden and fear over Mary's security increased. She took her to school and collected her after the end of the school day. Mary was beautiful with long dark hair, a complete replica of her mother. At home she was allowed to play only with girls and not boys. Nema was with her at every school function that she attended, even as she matured, she still followed her. One day Mary was so annoyed with her mother's over protectiveness that she spoke to her boldly and fearlessly. "Mama, why do you follow me everywhere as if I am in a den of lions?" she complained. "You are surely not in a den of lions but I can assure you that you are among wicked boys and men who are always ready to harm you" she said. "That is not how they appear to me", Mary retorted. Yes, some boys and men may be wicked but some of them are kind too", She argued. "Who is kind to you among the boys?"Nema asked with suspicion in her eyes. "Bamba is kind to me and some other boys are kind to me and I appreciate their kindness" She confessed. "What do they want from you? Tell me now, tell me something, I am waiting" she asked angrily. "They have not asked for anything; we talk and joke a lot" Mary explained. "Where exactly do you have your discussions" Nema asked again. "If you I ask you to stop talking to that Bamba what would be your response" She continued. "Mama, it would be difficult to malice a classmate for no reason whatsoever" She replied convincingly. Nema burst into tears when she recalled what had happened to her and feared the same thing may happen to her only daughter because she would not permit her to protect her the way she wanted. Mary was shocked to see her mother in tears over a simple matter. "Mama, tell me why you are crying over a very simple matter which we can solve easily" She asked. Then Nema explained to her exactly what happened to her in school with a boy called Patrick Konga (PK). "Please listen to me. Don't ever accept any invitation from any boy or man to his house no matter how kind they may be to you. They always have an agenda to tamper with you against your will" She warned. Mary grew up to hate boys and men because a boy spoiled her mother's chances of good education. She avoided boys and men as much as possible. But as she matured she reviewed her decisions because she found it unnecessary to keep away from boys and men just because her mother was abused by a boy many years ago. She decided to make a turnaround in her life. One day when she was returning home from school in a group with some girls, she stepped on a green snake. The fear and shock caused her to fall heavily on the ground. All the girls around her fled away, leaving her struggling to stand up. It was Bamba who rushed to the scene and killed the snake which had not gone far away. He returned and took her to the hospital on a Motorbike even before Nema knew. The nurses checked her and found no snake bite. After that incidence she became friendly to boys and Bamba became her close friend. When she explained to Nema how it all happened, Bamba featured prominently and Nema felt suspicious about him. When she learned later that a particular boy was flirting with Mary and she discovered the boy to be Bamba, she became furious. "Please stay away from him in school and tell him not come to my house for any reason whatsoever. If he does and I catch him, I will take the matter up with the school authorities" Nema threatened. "Mama what you are doing is not correct and whenever the authorities call me up for such matters, I will stop going to school and leave this environment" Mary threatened in turn. Nema looked up at her and saw desperation both in her voice and her facial expression. Henceforth she halted on the excessive monitoring.

For most of the time Sakayo was in the company of Kaye. They went to school together except when Sakayo was too late to join him. But surely they came home together. In an organized competition in class, Kaye was always on his side. In one such competition Sakayo posed a question to the other side: "There are ten birds in a tree and if a hunter shoots and kills one of them, how many will remain in the tree?" "Nine," said Posua and of all of them on the opposing side agreed with him. Slowly but surely, Sakayo announced that no bird will remain.

"Did you say ten birds and the hunter killed one? Obviously, Ten take away one is nine," argued Posua.

"Yes, ten take away one equals nine, but in the case of the ten birds, as soon as one bird is shot and killed, the nine will immediately fly away and no bird will remain in the tree", confirmed Sakayo. The class shouted and hit their tables in agreement with the answer.

Sakayo was hailed as the hero of the day. Kaye too felt proud being on his side. Two weeks later another competition was organized. Many questions were asked and the answers were provided by both sides. The question and answer that thrilled the class came again from Sakayo. "Think of any number and multiply that number by one hundred. Divide by the number you first thought of (that is dividing by fifty). Take away twenty five and the answer is twenty five," narrated Sakayo. The group that did the mathematics in one corner of the classroom shouted, "He got it, He got it". The group changed the number they thought of initially but Sakayo still got the answer right after many additions and subtractions. Posua was so impressed by the performance of his colleague that he decided to pay more attention to his books. Every afternoon he hid his books among the items that he took to the farm each day. Out there in the farm he read his books whenever he had the slightest opportunity because he wanted to do well in the class competitions and in his school work. He came from a small village called Tayandu not far away from Kayima. Initially, he walked to Kayima every school day until his parents made arrangements for him to stay with a friend in Kayima. He worked hard to make an impact at the class competitions. Even though he did not top his class, he made significant improvement in his school work and was recognized by his colleagues and the class teacher. Even Kaye could not figure out the technique behind this

Mathematical riddle. But he was quite sure Sakayo would teach him some day. He waited for weeks but Sakayo did not say anything about the riddle. He was anxious to know it and to use it in school as well. One day when they were alone, Kaye asked, "When are you going to teach me the technique of the Mathematical riddle?" "Whenever you are ready, said Sakayo smiling. "I am ready" said Kaye anxiously. "It is a simple technique," began Sakayo. "There are three points to remember. Firstly, you must ask them to think of any number. Secondly, suggest a number which they must multiply the unknown number by and thirdly, they must divide the product by the number they first thought of (The unknown number). You must concentrate on the number you suggested for the multiplication, as that will be the only number that will remain after dividing the product by the number they first thought of. For instance, let us consider 10 to be the number thought of, so if I say multiply by 50 and divide by the number original thought of, I am saying ten times fifty divided by ten which will give an answer of 50. In order words, the number which you suggest for multiplication is the number which you must concentrate on as you carry out your subtractions and divisions. This is to ensure you get the answer correctly." He concluded. "Do you understand it now?" asked Sakayo,

"Yes, I do," confirmed Kaye. "If you have understood it, prove that you have done so," requested Sakayo. "OK, think of any number. Multiply by Thirty and divide by the number you first thought of, take away fifteen, the answerer is fifteen" narrated Kaye.

"Good, the answer is correct. But you have to do more additions, subtractions and divisions to show that you know it well," advised Sakayo. When Kaye went home that evening he was very happy. He ate very little and kept some food hoping that Sakayo would come but he did not come. While he was on his bed he went over the instructions on the riddle. When there was a doubt anywhere in the procedure, he got up and worked out a sum to ensure that he did not forget the principles. He wanted to show that he too was a good mathematician. Kaye went over the example many times in the day. When the day for the competition came, the children were quite ready to display their skills. Kaye represented his group instead of Sakayo, whilst Posua represented the other group. The winner of the competition was normally the group that provided correct answers to questions and above all provided unique riddles. The hero was the one who answered more questions. Kaye did very well. He answered his questions very well and before the end of the competition he brought in "think of any number riddle". He worked through different numbers and got the answers right. The entire class hailed him whenever he got each answer right. At the end of the competition he was declared the hero. Think of any number riddle was still a challenge to the entire school. In and out of school Sakayo and Kaye were considered great mathematicians. They showed interest in Mathematics and that improved their grades in every test or examination in school.

Chairman Entona Kebbie was considered a useful man in the society. He was respected for having worked with white men in a big company from where he was able to establish himself in Kayima. In court he was always on time and strict in dealing with every matter brought before him. He gave right to where it belonged and avoided unnecessary adjournments. He tried to make his life as good as it used to be in Yengema. He organized the palm wine drinking club because called Bassama because there were no bars in Kayima. He spent a lot of his time to get the club working by putting in place an effective executive. When he got an executive in place, he allowed them to function in accordance with their constitution. The Financial Secretary collected the monthly contributions and distributed to members their membership cards. And within a short time the membership grew and so did the revenue. The Social Secretary also made concrete arrangements with some palm wine tappers which required them to supply quality palm wine to the club on a daily basis. He received the palm wine from the tappers every day and ensured it was of good quality before presenting it to the group. He also ensured that pepper soup was served together with the palm wine every evening. Entona did not take any positions in the club as he was the chief patron. He left his house for the court house very early every day to look into any matter before him before the court sittings commenced. When the court house closed down for the day, he remained in the office to write his reports. He would then rush home to have his lunch and he would spend some time with his family and later join his club members for the evening entertainment. His engagements remained the same throughout the year.

Soui Nanpanneh was the chief of Sandoh Chiefdom. He ruled his people with wisdom. He relied on the history, culture, and the chiefdom's administrative rules and regulations to administer judgments. For him no matter was simple. He gave a lot of his time to all disputes brought before him and once he made a decision, it was final and he stood by it. He always insisted on a change of attitude and behavior for all those who were guilty of breaking the laws. When he had a right in a matter over another man, he would not accept fines initially; neither would he say the matter was ended. Only a change of attitude would bring the matter to an end, otherwise he would bring the matter up again at any time no matter how long it had taken and punish the culprit appropriately. He was a man, whose matter did not end, thereby earning himself the name "Nanpanneh", which meant trouble in the Kono language. He had a passion for news of any kind and that made his house a center where men, women and children met. One day Sakayo decided to test whether Soui Nanpaneh was as wise as he was widely thought to be. Early one morning he caught a butterfly alive and decided to use it to test him. He decided he would ask him whether the butterfly in his hand was alive or dead. If he said it was dead, then he would release it alive. But if he said it was alive, then he would squeeze it to death and present it to him, to prove that he was wrong. That morning he went to his house alone and found him with his councilors. "Good morning chief" he said "Good morning little boy. Can I help you?" asked the chief. "Chief, here is a butterfly in my hand. I want you to say whether it is alive or dead", he said. The chief was amazed and stood quietly for some time thinking aloud. Then he looked at him from head to toe and wondered what he wanted. After analysing the issue, he knew what to tell him. "Little boy, the butterfly's survival is absolutely under your control; if it lives it means you have decided that it must live, but if it dies you have decided it as well" said the chief with confidence.

Sakayo giggled, opened his hand and the butterfly flew away. "Now, you have decided that it must live, that is why you have released it alive" said the chief. "Mark this little boy, he has a potential to be a leader because he is wise", remarked the chief. He then took a coin from his pocket and gave it to Sakayo. From that day Sakayo believed that the chief had wisdom.

Chapter Five

Suku in the Tree

Suku was the son of Soui Nanpanneh, the Chief. He liked Sakayo because he gave him some sweet wild fruits often. He always looked for him whenever he walked around. And Sakayo never disappointed him because for most of the time his pockets had some fruits.

One day Suku found a bunch of mangoes on a branch which was high up in the tree, at the edge of the town. The mango season was almost at an end and mangoes found at that time of the year were precious and valued. Suku did not tell anybody but decided to climb and harvest them. He had never climbed a tree as big and tall like that one but he was desperate for the mangoes. He took his time and climbed and arrived at the branch that had the mangoes. They were still far away from him. He then stepped on a branch that ran parallel to the branch with the mangoes, with his other foot on the main branch. Half way through the distance the parallel branch broke under his weight as it had dried up and became weak. He staggered and sat on the main branch and held firmly onto a small branch. The branch moved up and down with him due to the displacement caused by the broken branch. He could neither shout nor cry. He tightened his grip on the branch until it became steady again. But he could neither move forward nor return due to the missing branch. He looked down and realized that if he fell from that point he may not survive. He sat down there thinking of what to do. Finally, he decided to shout at the top of his voice so that he could be heard from afar. He shouted and shouted but he did not get any

57

reply. Then he changed his mind and cried aloud making a despairing appeal: "I am falling, I am falling." A young girl heard him and ran away from the scene in fear. She came and sat close to her mother speechless but she noticed the uneasiness in her.

"What is the matter with you?" She asked. "There is somebody crying in the tree at the back of the house" she said. She got up and ran to the scene. She looked up but could not see anybody. Then she heard a voice shouting "I am falling," and immediately she saw Suku high up in the tree. "Suku, can't you come down?" she asked. Suku looked down and saw her.

"Aunty Sia, I can't come down by myself. I am trapped and my grip is failing me slowly" he said weeping. Sia ran to the chief's compound which was a short distance away. She found a crowd around him. "Suku is in the tree. He cannot come down by himself. Please come to his aid." She said in a hurry. The crowd moved quickly to the scene and saw Suku on the branch. When he saw his father, he wept bitterly. "Father please act quickly to save my life. I will never climb a tree again," he said between sobs. The event stunned the chief and put him in a worrisome state of mind. Suddenly, a volunteer was already climbing the tree to rescue him. He arrived at the point but the boy was out of his reach. And if he stepped on the branch it may collapsed under their weight. The chief saw the risk and asked him to come down without delay. "Hold fast unto the branch," the chief said to his son. Meanwhile, he appointed some strong men to stand directly under him in case his hands got tired and fell over. They stood underneath and concentrated on his hand movements and prepared to catch him if he fell over suddenly. A group of women came out with fishing nets and some strong men held them up two to one across the space directly under him and urged him to release the tree and fall over. "Drop down," they commanded him. Suku looked upon the nets and released his grip on the branch little by little. But when he looked down the second time, fear came upon him and he could not drop down. "Drop down and we shall hold you up in the nets" shouted the crowd but he could not. Two ladders were brought and joined together but they were not long enough to reach him and the idea was dropped and the ladders were taken away quickly. The entire township gathered under the tree but without a solution to bring Suku down. The situation became serious as the boy cried for help as his grip was loosening on the branch. So many pieces of advice made the chief indecisive, not knowing which one would provide the required solution. Sakayo came to the scene and saw Suku on the branch and told the man next to him that he could bring Suku down safely. "Get away, you underfed little boy. You think you are better than all of us here" Declared man. "If he says he can do it, why not give him a trial?" said another man who took him seriously. He went to the chief and reported what the little boy said concerning bringing Suku down safely. The chief looked at him and recalled that he was the court chairman's son who brought a butterfly to his house one morning. He remembered him as a clever boy and asked a few questions before giving him the go ahead. "Can you do it?" he asked him. "Yes, I can do it, if you can get me a long cord and a log about his weight" he said. Within minutes two long cords and three logs were brought. Sakayo examined the cords and the logs and selected one cord and a log. He made a loop at the edge of the cord and tied the other edge to the log. He climbed beyond the branch where Suku sat. He sent down the loop to him and asked him to wear it and fasten it on his trunk, precisely under his arms.

Suku obeyed every instruction. His eyes shone with joy with Sakayo with him in the tree.

He then passed the cord between two branches forming a fork in the tree. He came down to his level and encouraged him to walk towards him. Suku got up slowly trembling and then sat down because his legs could not support him. He was encouraged by the crowd to be brave and to walk to him. It was a breathtaking moment with a large crowd watching the tree with full attention. Even a fly could be detected flying from that tree or if a needle fell from it, it could be heard. Suku looked around and found some of his friends who encouraged him further to move towards Sakayo and be saved, and he got some additional strength and courage. He lifted his left leg that proved to be more reluctant to move. Again, he got up slowly and took the first step with his right foot, and then his left foot, after much delay. He took a few steps, slipped and fell over but the cord kept him suspended in the air. And as he struggled, the log moved up slowly whilst he descended slowly until he hit the ground. There was a thunderous uproar as the crowd saw Suku on the ground. A lady sang a song and the crowd picked up the tune and sang. The entire day was spent in dancing and eating. Sakayo was on the shoulder of a strong man in a big crowd and there was merriment in every corner of the Town.

An old woman who did not know what had happened came out of her house to find out the reason for the up and down movement. Old age had kept her out of public life and most events that happened in the town, even those of interest to her she missed. On that particular day she was curious to ask people what happened. As she stood outside her house she saw a group of young women and asked them what had happened in the town but nobody said anything to her. She asked another man running to the chief's house but he too went away without saying anything to her. She waited until she saw another group of people walking past her house and she decided to ask a question that would force them to say something. "Whose son has been murdered?" she asked. "God forbid, nobody was murdered. The chief's son was trapped in a tree but he has been brought down safely", said one of the men. The old woman was happy that she knew exactly what was happening in the town and went back to her house satisfied

Chapter Six

The Missionary

It was in the thick of the celebrations when a white missionary, Mr. Anderson came to see the chief. He found him in a joyful mood over the rescue of his son from the tree. The chief took him to the tree where he saw the handiwork of a little boy that saved his son. He was curious and requested to see the boy who saved him. Sakayo was brought before him immediately and he asked him a few questions and requested to see his parents too. The chief didn't know what to give to him as a gift for saving his son but Mr. Anderson intervened quickly and asked Sakayo a simple question: "Between Education and Money which one would you choose as a compensation for saving the chief's son? "Education" he answered. The chief immediately sent a message to Mr. Kebbie and his wife about Mr. Anderson's visit the next day which concerned his son Sakayo. It was indeed an unusual visit, especially when it concerned a white man. The couple, although a little bit apprehensive, got themselves prepared in their own way. Nema prepared some cassava leaves with goat meat whilst Entona got a gallon of good palm wine from his club. The couple was at home when Mr. Anderson came to see them and introduced himself as soon as he arrived home. "My name is John Anderson, a Christian Missionary from the US, assigned to your Region. I was with the chief a few days ago and he told me quite a lot about your son by the name of Sakayo. I was very impressed about the way he saved Suku's life. And when we asked him to choose between money and education for compensation, he preferred education. I am here to seek your permission so that I can make an input in his education" he appealed to them. Entona got up and shook his hand firmly in support of his suggestion. But before he sat down Nema got up and whispered a message in his ears and the two then moved quickly into an inner room for consultations. "Entona, tell this man to give us a few days so that we can discuss the issue properly. It concerns a life and it obviously requires more time." She told him. Entona accepted her suggestion as reasonable. He therefore came out of the meeting and expressed his appreciation to Mr. Anderson for his good intention and plans to help educate his son. However, he told him that his family would meet on the issue the next day and then asked him to come after two days by which time the necessary decisions would have been taken. He signaled to Nema to serve Mr Anderson some food and drinks but he said he was OK and thanked them for the gesture explaining that he had some food at the chief's House. At end of the meeting Mr. Anderson got up, shook their hands and promised to be back soon.

The next morning Aunty Nema went shopping in the central market. It was a Monday and a market day involving many villages. Various food items were displayed in and around the market, with a large number of people moving from one table to other buying or negotiating prices. She bought a few items and walked through the crowd towards Yarya road and walked straight into the house of Mondeh, a friend of Entona. "I am happy I have found you at home" she told him. "What is the matter?" he asked. "Your friend is about to give away his son to a Missionary. He does not even know the man well enough, yet he is prepared to risk it. Can you beat that? Please do something about it without him knowing that I complained", she begged and tried to make her visit very brief so that nobody related to Entona saw her in the house.

"I think Entona will discuss the matter with me, and surely I will give some pieces of advice concerning that. Anyway, thank you for calling and goodbye" said Mondeh, as Aunty Nema stepped out of the door.

Back home Entona saw the need to discuss the full implications of allowing the boy to go with Mr. Anderson. He began the discussion by asking her a question. "Nema, what do you think about sending Sakayo away with Mr. Anderson?" He asked.

"First of all, are we incapable of taking care of him? I think we are doing well in that respect. But he is your son and whatever you decide for him it is well and good" She said.

"But let me warn you beforehand that when I shall have my own son, he will not stay with a missionary. He will grow up in this house under my supervision." She added angrily.

"Do you have any experience with missionaries? I don't think you know them well enough" He said, confused. "No, I don't have any experience with them. But I know how to bring up a child, and that is exactly what the missionary will do when Sakayo goes to stay with him, nothing more. The plate of rice that I give to him out here is the same he will receive from Mr. Anderson. If he gets more, that will be equal to over feeding and will affect his growth negatively". She explained. "I just want to inform you that missionaries are genuine and kind people. In my early secondary school days, three of my colleagues were taken by a missionary. Today, all of them are highly educated and in good jobs. I have no doubt that Mr. Anderson will help Sakayo to be highly educated as well", he tried to convince her. "Please don't misunderstand me. I don't have any objections to his going with him. Try to be man enough to take the final decision," she said. Entona could not resolve Sakayo's issue with her. She was adamant about the fact that she was capable of taking care of him and that nobody had any reason to send him away to a missionary. But he was convinced that Sakayo would get the education he said he needed and nobody should alter the path he had chosen.

The evening found him at Bassama Club, where he and his friends had spent one hour drinking and eating. After much entertainment, he brought up Sakayo's issue for discussion. It became a lively debate in the Club. Mondeh was clearly on the side of Nema. He tried to convince the members that children should be brought up by their parents because that gave them the opportunity to know them, their relatives and friends and cultivate love for them. He said a child brought up outside the home would not be a normal child, especially if he failed to get his parents' love. He therefore encouraged Entona to listen to Nema's suggestions.

Other members argued that children should be brought up anywhere, as long as they are under very good care, and they are in contact with their parents, no matter how poor they may be. They said that Entona should release the child to the missionary who had promised to give him a very good education. They cited many examples of children from distant villages who were taken by missionaries and who became top civil servants. The argument became heated and Entona asked for a vote on the issue. All the members in favor of Nema's suggestions were asked to put up their hands and they were 30. And all those in favor of the missionary were also asked to put up their hands and they were 34. The matter was decided according to the votes. Mr. Anderson would travel with Sakayo whenever he turned up. All the members accepted the outcome of their votes and continued to entertain themselves as a popular music played in the background.

Back home Nema was furious when she learnt that the Club endorsed the idea that Sakayo should go with the missionary. The following day she called Sakayo aside and tried to get his reaction about his going with the Missionary, "Are you happy that your father has decided that the missionary should take you along?" she asked. "I don't know about it Aunty" he said timidly. "Your teacher told me that you are clever. But you cannot remember what I told you just a few days ago. Didn't I ask you to run away from home on a temporary basis on the day the missionary is here?" she reminded him. "Yes, you did but I don't know where to go. I don't know anybody in Yarya, Kaminkudu or Foemankadu" he told her. "Look here, tomorrow you must go to Yarya and ask for the Kasegbama family and stay with them until the missionary comes and goes away" she instructed. The next morning Entona got all Sakayo's belongings into a small suitcase and got it ready for the journey. And within a short time Mr. Anderson pulled up in a pick up van in front of the house. Entona received him and brought him into his parlor where Nema sat by the door. She shook hands with him and sat back in the chair with a smile on her face whilst Entona went in and out of the house looking for Sakayo but he was nowhere to be found. What was he going to say to Mr. Anderson? He wondered. He could not find the words to explain his absence even after spending some good time thinking about it. Finally, he got out of his room and pretended that he was with his friend Kaye and immediately sent somebody there. But his mind was unsettled about his whereabouts. Could it be that she had connived with him to sabotage the trip? He wondered what may have happened. It was in the midst of his torment that Biango, a Motorbike rider brought Sakayo back home and packed his Motorbike right in front of his house. When he peeped out he saw them, he could not believe his eyes. Both of them came into the house and Biango asked Entona's permission to speak to him privately. He went with the two into his bedroom and listened to their story. "I found him wandering towards Yarya but he could not give me a convincing reason for going there. So I decided to bring him back home" said Biango. "Thank you for your effort and wisdom. We shall talk about this strange behavior some other time" Said Entona. Biango then said goodbye and moved into the parlor and walked through the door to his Motorbike which was parked in front of the house. He sat on it and moved, leaving a trail of black smoke behind him and a cracking sound from the exhaust pipe. Entona and Sakayo joined Anderson and Nema in the parlor. It was very quiet in the parlor but eye contact was prominent. Nema stared at Sakayo and at Anderson, whilst Entona stared at Nema and then at Sakayo.

Mr. Anderson waited patiently but also stared at each of them to get a feel of what was happening. Finally, Entona broke the silence and asked Sakayo to look straight at him.

"Mr. Anderson is taking you along to give you good education. Are you willing to go with him?" he asked.

Sakayo stared at Nema for a long time and could not utter a single word.

"Sakayo, are you willing to go?" He asked again with more emphasis on the word go.

"Yes" he said timidly looking in the direction of Mr. Anderson and avoiding Nema's gaze.

"Mr. Anderson, here is Sakayo. The family supports you fully for your desire to educate him. Don't spare the rod when he behaves abnormally and keep me informed about any negative developments that may affect your plan for him." said Entona. Mr. Anderson got up and held Sakayo by his right hand and turned to Entona and said: "I will do my level best, God willing." He assured the couple. Entona went into his room and brought out his suitcase and led the way to the pickup van. Mr. Anderson took the driver's seat whilst he sat in the passenger's seat.

When the engine started, Sakayo looked out through the window searching for his friend Kaye. He stood in one corner of the verandah, tears running down his cheeks. He wanted him to stay but he could not stop him. He felt that his departure would affect his life both at home and in school and he was quite sure he would be walking up and down alone for a long time to come. That was why he could not resist tears running down his cheeks at the final moment of his departure. And as the vehicle moved slowly, Sakayo saw him and waved at him frantically with a clenched fist and a broad smile on his face. Kaye was completely amazed because he waved with a clenched fist with a broad smile on his face. Was he indicating superiority right at the beginning of his journey? This could not be the case because he was such a humble and honest friend who did not show any difference between him and other friends. What then was he symbolizing by his clenched fist and the broad smile at the moment when he was shedding tears? Could he be talking about success, and whose success could it be?

Whatever he meant by his clenched fist was going to be for the benefit of all his friends, and obviously I would be the number one person judging from the strong bonds of our friendship.

He wiped his tears and walked to his house feeling good that his friend had had his turn and his was on the way. When Sakayo left the school, Posua and Kaye battled it out for leadership of the class competitions.

Mr. Anderson and Sakayo made the journey to Koidu town through many villages. It took about an hour. They drove through many streets and arrived at a place called Paul Square. It was a very short street indeed with about four houses on each side of the street. The southern end of this street went as far down as 300 meters and touched the river Kaisambo. Diamond miners had cut this river into many parts like a snake found in the home of a farmer. The part of the river facing Paul Square was a pool of dirty water completely deprived of taking its course downstream. They drove right down the street and arrived at the last house on the right hand side of the street. It was Mr. Anderson's house. Sakayo was well received by Mrs. Anderson. She gave him a key to his own room, which had a comfortable bed, a study table and Bible. He settled down quickly in his new home. The next day he got up early and looked for what to do. There was not much to be done. Nevertheless, he went to Mrs. Anderson and asked about what chore there was that he could do in the morning. He was shown one or two chores which could not last beyond twenty minutes. He was told that there was a paid person who cleaned and laundered, and there was a cook. Within a few days he was tested and placed in class six in The Methodist Church School, Koidu town. He liked his new school, although he found himself among much younger boys than himself. He took courage because there were a handful of boys who were as big and tall as him. At home he had more time for his school work and hunger became a thing of the past. He had his food on time and had enough time to play football in an open space close to the river. Within two weeks he made friends in his neighborhood who were already in secondary school but three of them were with him in the same primary school which he attended. Despite age and class differences, Sakayo played football with them on a small piece of land that Paul Square afforded for games. Sometimes they went to other parts of the town to play football with the knowledge of their parents or guardians. His conversations with his new friends in secondary school brought a lot of excitement to him. They always spoke good things about Jaiama Secondary School where some of them attended. They spoke about the beauty of their Boarding Home and the way they enjoyed their lives there. They were in Koidu town for some of the weekends to receive pocket money for use in school. He grew to love the school and decided he would be in the Boarding Home the following academic year and he did not waste any time in making his request known to the Andersons that Jaiama secondary school was his choice for the National Primary School Examinations. His request was endorsed and he was encouraged to work harder. The desire to be part of the Boarding Home kept him busy at his books. He revised Mathematics and

English Language often and answered many past papers in all the subjects. Sometimes his friends in secondary school came to his room to assist him with whatever he had difficulty with. He worked consistently and rested a month to the examinations. He was confident that he would pass with good grades because he had done all that he needed to do. And barely after a month he took the examinations and confidently assured the Andersons that he would pass with flying colors based on the answers that he provided in the examinations. He thought about them so much that one night he dreamt the result were released and he was told he got 300 out of 500 marks. When he woke up the next morning he was not happy about the dream because as far as he was concerned the mark was low. He enquired and found out that the preceding year's best candidate for Jaiama secondary school scored 330 marks. He did not take the dream that serious because he knew what he had done. He decided to wait patiently without showing any anxiety, but that was almost impossible because his friends kept on coming to visit him. And each time they were together they discussed the examinations and consequently the results. One day Mr. Anderson came home very early and found him in a Bible lesson with Mrs. Anderson. "Sakayo, congratulations, you have passed with very good grades, and your interview is on the 6th September," Said Mr. Anderson. He ran out of the lesson with joy and with great expectations. He went straight to meet Mr. Anderson who stood at the door, took a paper from his hand bag and took out his reading glasses to make sure it was the correct paper. He looked at it and confirmed that it was. He then handed it over to Mrs. Anderson who was also curious to know the grades. At that crucial moment

Sakayo kept looking up at the leaflet that hid his grades. He wanted to know them immediately so that he could start celebrating. But within a short time Mrs. Anderson calmly told him that all the grades were very good after reading through the one page document and then shook his hand firmly. But he was still anxious to know the actual grades but he had to be polite to allow Mrs. Anderson to satisfy her curiosity first. Finally, the paper was handed over to him and indeed the grades were good with an average of 380. He was happy because he was able to fulfill his promise to the Andersons.

With a broad smile on his face he thanked the Andersons for being so kind to him and then asked Mr. Anderson to inform his father about his success to Jaiama secondary School. He nodded his head indicating that he would do it. Mr Anderson took him for the Interview and found that he was already accepted and placed in the best stream. Two weeks later Jaiama Secondary school re-opened on the 20th of September and the parents of both new and old pupils were all prepared to take their children to school. Those who had to go to the Boarding Home needed more preparation. They had to buy many items and a chop box into which normally went various food items. The Andersons took Sakayo to the market to buy his books and other items that he may need in school. They went through Sandoh Street and drove up to Provincial Enterprises located at Gbongbor Street, where they bought all the books that he needed for school. They moved to the site of Gbessan River which had been transformed into a big market and bought two pairs of crepe shoes, ten shirts and six pairs of trousers. They also bought a big chop box and filled it with assorted food items. Sakayo was very happy about the two crepe shoes. He decided immediately that one pair would be for school and the other for football. He was not a good player by any standards but he had a passion for football. Every day he played football either around Paul Square or along the sand close to Kaisambo River. Playing near the river required somebody to swim into the river each time the ball missed its target and fell into the river. There was always a third team waiting while two teams played on. In the second team there was always a volunteer who would swim quickly into the river and collect the ball.

The next day Mr. Anderson packed Sakayo's luggage into the pick up van and drove towards Jaiama Town, which was 15 Kilometres away. When he arrived in the Town he knew already where to look for the school. He drove straight to the Police Station and then turned left. Within a few seconds he was in front of the office. He went into the office and spoke to a short and heavily built man. He was the Bursar and he introduced himself as Mr. Karkamoe.

Mr. Anderson paid all the fees that Sakayo had to pay for the year and then took him to the Boarding Home, which was about 100 meters away from the office. Mr. Anderson spoke to Mr. Koatambo, the Boarding Home master for a long time after which he produced a white envelope that he handed over to Sakayo and drove off to town.

Mr. Koatambo then asked Sakayo to follow him. They went through a long corridor and arrived at a building and then stopped suddenly. "This is Yamba dormitory and you are going to be resident here" he said. They walked into the building and went to a bed in one corner of the hall.

"This is your bed. By tomorrow you will be told how to behave here" he told him and then asked him to bring his luggage inside. Sakayo went swiftly across the long corridor and brought his chop box, and then his suitcase and school bag. He opened the suitcase and took out a bed sheet and pillow cases. He dressed his bed and sat on it and looked around the building. It was a big building with many beds in the hall. The beds were well arranged with a passage in between them. What amazed him most was that some of the beds were double, with one bed sitting on top of another. He wished he had the upper bed. But suddenly he realized that he could fall over very easily whenever he made any mistakes. He decided the best choice had been made for him. Adjacent to Yamba dormitory was another big building with similar arrangements. That building turned out to be Turner dormitory. As he waited on his bed he fell asleep. He was awoken by a group of boys who entered the building with a lot of noise that woke him up immediately. They entered the hall and walked directly to him with enthusiasm and inquisitive attitudes towards him. He got up quickly and sat on the edge of the bed and pretended to be concentrating on something. "What is your name and class please?" asked one of the boys.

"My name is Sakayo and I am a Form One pupil" he told them calmly. "Greener, Greener" shouted the group of boys together. "Welcome to Jaiama School. By 13th October we shall get rid of the chlorophyll in you" they told him emphatically and went to their beds. Some of them cleaned their crepe shoes and others ironed their uniforms in preparation for School the next day. Sakayo wondered what they meant by all the statements they made. Why did they refer to him as a "Greener"? Was he so primitive and unfit in their midst? What did they mean by chlorophyll? These questions made him uneasy and kept him moody for most of the day. But by the end of the day he learnt that a 'Greener' was a fresher to Jaiama secondary school and chlorophyll was the substance that made a green leaf green. He was told that he had to undergo some drills to get him to adapt to the Jaiama Secondary School traditions and cultures, and get rid of pettiness and laziness from his former way of doing things.

He also learnt that 13th October was the school's foundation day celebrations and it was a big occasion for both the present and past pupils of the school.

Entona and Nema slept over the differences between them concerning Sakayo's departure. But there was a noticeable physical difference in the home. There was a shortage of firewood and water. The house was dirty and its surroundings were bushy. Sometimes Entona wore clothes to work which were not properly ironed because he hadn't enough time to do it himself.

The problem was compounded when Nema showed signs of being pregnant but the pregnancy never developed beyond the first two months. Life became difficult for her and she resorted to a strike action. She refused to cook until an assistant was found. They went without water for two days and on the third day he went to Bondu, Sakayo's aunt and explained the problem that he had with his wife after Sakayo's departure. He then made a request for Kaye to help with some of the chores, especially fetching fire wood during the weekends and promised that he would contribute handsomely to whatever he took to school as lunch on a daily basis. He informed her that he was already familiar with the home, being Sakayo's close friend. Bondu listened patiently and turned to Kaye who sat close by. "Are you willing and able to help him", she asked. "Yes, I am willing to help out", he replied smiling. "We are bringing up our children for each other in the community. I am OK with his decision and I will keep reminding him so that he does not forget what has been agreed", she assured him. From that day he took over Sakayo's chores. This was made possible because he had very little to do at home and he considered his input as some help to Sakayo, his close friend. From that day he went into the nearby bushes around to identify fire wood in preparation of his new assignment. And indeed he found a reasonable stock of it close to the town. Every weekend he went out there to cut fire wood and he was never found wanting until he passed his examinations for Yengema Secondary School and left Kayima.

Sakayo's first day in Jaiama Secondary School was full of excitement. The first teacher that they had that morning was the Geography teacher. He entered the classroom cautiously and sat in front of the class. He introduced himself as Mr. Lahai and he had with him a pen and a notebook. He told the class that his topic for that day was self-introduction. As he spoke to them, he struggled to get his words out quickly. And when he got them out he made sure he repeated them to ensure that everyone understood what he meant. Truly, he stammered but tried as much as possible to conceal it away from the pupils but some clever pupils noticed the persistent up and down movement of his hands. Then row by row he asked each pupil to stand up and give a brief history about himself and his family in English. It was the rule that the speaker gave his name before commencing the narrative. He took down the name in his notebook and listened keenly to what was said. When a grammatical mistake was made he noted it whilst the class shouted 'bullet', as every grammatical error was considered a bullet from a gun. Before he completed the exercise there was a lot of laughter in the classroom as more bullets were released. He then compiled the mistakes on the blackboard and worked with the pupils to provide the correct answers which he displayed on the blackboard for all to copy. He informed them that English was crucial for the study of all subjects. Before he left the classroom he asked some particular students to see him immediately. The class suspected that those students who had released the bullets were the ones the teacher wanted to see.

The next lesson was French. The teacher entered the classroom when the pupils were busy copying what Mr. Lahai had left on the blackboard. When they had finished he was still standing in one corner of the classroom and urged them to copy the notes quickly so he could start his lesson. He was a short man, well dressed with a constant smile on his face.

He introduced himself as Mr. Lebbie but later the pupils found out that his nickname was "Termagant". They wanted to know what "Termagant" meant but none dared to do any investigations for fear that he may find out and punish them. Definitely, some teachers and some senior students called him "Tamacant" but he did not like pupils to use it at all. He was therefore prepared to punish any pupil who insisted on calling him his nick name.

He started the lesson by listing many verbs on the blackboard and selected the verb to be and conjugated it.

Then he asked the class to repeat after him the various persons of the conjugated verb. After quite a lot of exercise he then asked them to read them out individually, which resulted into an uncontrollable laughter in the classroom. The words were strange and the sounds were somehow funny. Despite the initial difficulties encountered with pronunciations, many of the pupils seemed to like the subject. They held onto the French textbook long after the lesson to listen to themselves reading French. One pupil earned himself the name 'Kwaku' after one of the characters in the prescribed French text book for Form One. His real name was Sirus but the name 'Kwaku' became so popular to the extent that the name Sirus almost disappeared, as all his classmates referred to him as Kwaku, in and outside the classroom. As October 13th drew closer, Sakayo decided to learn the school's song and motto. Within a few days he crammed the song but had some difficulties with the motto simply because it was in Latin. It read "Appetens Veri Recti Tenax" which means "Strive for truth and stand for the right". He read it over trying to find the best way to remember it. Then he realized that Tenax looked like the word Tenap which means Stand up in Krio. The similarity helped him a lot to remember the Motto. He made it a habit to sing the song and recite the motto whenever he was alone and when nobody was paying attention to him. That normally happened when he was away to Konda to buy basic items like soap or sugar. He would sing aloud and march as if the day had come. With a lot of practice, he was confident that come October 13th he would not be found wanting. He was therefore quite sure nobody was going to punish him for not knowing the song and motto. But he didn't know all that was required of a fresher, and so he entertained some fear, especially if he fell into the hands of a desperate old boy at the drills. He was told by some non-fresher's that some students wept at the end of the exercise for various mistreatments. But at the same time some others enjoyed it so much that they wanted to be part of it all. On the issue of October 13th, his mind was not quite settled. At some moments he felt he would participate fully, but at other times he felt he should pretend to be sick so that he would escape the entire celebrations. But in his class there were some boys much younger than him who seemed not to be afraid at all. In fact, they wanted to go through it so that the following year they too would qualify to deal with the future non-freshers. He too decided to participate fully no matter the consequences. He got his crepe shoes ready for the trip and prepared two khaki shorts to be worn on that day as a protection against whips that may land on his buttocks. He enjoyed all aspects of school life until 13th October, the D-day. He was forced to wake up at 5 am to join a long queue of Fresher's for the cross-country drill. It was dark but they had to be there or suffer hasher punishments. As more Freshers joined the queue from both the Boarding Home and the day students, the open air school Assembly was packed full like a normal school day. There were many non-freshers playing supervisory roles along the Queues with little correctional whips in their hands. As long as a student was in the second form or higher he became a supervisor provided he himself had undergone the drills. They walked around pompously and punished the slightest anomaly. They waited in the single file until the prefect in charge appeared on the scene with his regimental language and posture. He was tall and looked like any teacher. But he told them that he was one of the prefects in Form Five science, the most respected class of the school. And everybody accepted what he said because if he had any way to prove that somebody doubted what he had said, his punishment would be multiplied. He then gave his orders that would guide the team throughout the journey. He asked them to be quiet and there was absolute silence as he walked along the queue to see that the line was in perfect order. And indeed, immediate adjustments were made that straightened out the crooked bits. Then he asked them to sing the school's song after three counts. And after three counts, a full blast of the song was sung from the beginning to the end of the queue. The fresher's sang and the non-freshers were pleased with the rhythm. They had learnt the song and the motto long before 13th October because they knew that if they did not, they could be punished and embarrassed. They sang the school's song for nearly five minutes and then read the motto over and over, with its translation in English. "APPETENS VERI RECTI TENAX" - "STRIVE FOR TRUTH AND STAND FOR THE RIGHT".

Two teachers were seen around probably to ensure that nobody did anything in excess. But they were too few to make any significant impact. The Prefect then ordered a forward movement and immediately the long queue started to move forward quickly. They went right across the entire Jaiama town through Gbogbora Road, running and singing and heading towards Njala town. It was a rough and bumpy road and they could not tell how far they were going but zealous non- freshers were quite determined to go as far as possible. They ran at a reasonable speed and sang many other songs as directed by the Prefect. When they arrived in Njala, they went round the town singing and clapping their hands. Even though it was very early many people came out of the homes to see what was happening, and they were amazed to see so many students in their town that morning. They stayed there for a brief moment and began their return journey the next few minutes. They had run a long distance and they had become weak and tired. Some of the students had developed blisters on their soles despite their strong pairs of crepe shoes. That made the return journey much more difficult. But they had to cope with the pace of the prefect, whether that meant running or walking fast. They arrived at the school compound hungry and thirsty but they had to be in the single file until they were told what to do next. When they were finally released, it was joy to everyone. The experience was different for each student, depending on where he was in the line.

Sakayo was almost in the middle and a non-fresher's whip landed on his feet once for slowing down. The accounts of other students were much more serious but they all bore the burden of the exercise with the hope that the following year they too would be the non-freshers.

The ceremony was climaxed by a football match between the old boys and the current pupils, which ended in a goalless draw. The football match was followed by a ball dance in the town's Court Barray. It was a well attended dance which further strengthened the Jaiama Old Students Association (JOSA).

Entona received a letter from Mr. Anderson which had two crucially important messages: Firstly, that Sakayo passed his examinations and had been admitted at Jaiama Secondary School and that he had settled his school fees and other expenses. Secondly, that he had been recalled to work in his country, and was leaving the country in the next two months. The letter brought some joy as far as his son was concerned, but news about his departure also caused his head to ache. But he took courage in a sentence at the end of the letter which read: "I will do my best for Sakayo." He arrived home very late that day and waited until the next morning when he brought out the letter and read it out to Nema. "Why are you reading it to me? Does it concern me at all?" She exclaimed. "Oh yes, it concerns you because if Mr. Anderson goes away I am duty bound to support him with the income which I am earning, which happens to be yours as well. Don't you think you are concerned?" he said.

"What is going to be Betty's role in all of this? She must contribute half of whatever is going to be the expenditure. She must learn to suffer now for tomorrow's enjoyment. If she does not contribute I will not be part of the deal" She emphasized. "I don't even know where she is," He said. "It is in your best interest to locate her now and get her to contribute," Nema repeated.

Entona realized that if he continued answering back the discussion may be diverted to other issues and may lead to a quarrel. Therefore he kept quiet and looked on sheepishly as Nema made her accusing comments.

Biango rode his Motorbike up a rugged hill at the side of which was the town called Kasay-chaindedu. He was carrying a pillion who had hired him from Kayima. It was hardly noticeable from a distance as it was completely shielded from the sun light by the leaves of many tall trees which encircled the entire town. He arrived there by mid- day and it was cool and calm out there like the early hours of the morning, but in the evening it got dark quickly. As he waited for the pillion to get his load together, he saw Betty on the verandah of the house next to where he was. He walked up to her, hoping that she too would recognize him, but she did not recognize him at all. She looked at him up and down without making any comments and she searched her mind to come out with a name but she could not. Biango smiled and introduced himself. "You are Betty, Entona's wife and I am Biango, the Motorbike rider in Kayima", he said. "Oh yes, you are Biango indeed. If you were standing by your Motorbike I would have recognized you and call your name instantly", she said laughing. "I am quite well and I am going away any moment from now", he informed her. "Do you know anything about my son Sakayo", he asked. "I know that he is now in Jaiama Secondary School. I have been there twice on hire but I did not attempt to see him because the pillion asked me to take him to a village outside Jaiama town. But I have another trip for Jaiama tomorrow. I will try and see him, especially so if you have something for him or a message", he explained. "Good, I have some money for him. Let me bring it out immediately", she said and ran to her room and returned with a sealed envelope. "Please give him this envelope containing some money for his lunch and tell him that I love him with all my heart and that I shall pay him a visit someday", she said. Biango received the envelope and walked back to his Motorbike and placed it in his travelling bag and returned to her quickly. "Biango, I have not been able to see Sakayo all these years simply because he lived with white missionaries who do not know that I am his mother. Besides, I don't know the instructions they have received from Entona concerning who should be allowed to see him. I found it extremely difficult to confront those white men on that issue. This is why I have not seen him ever since", she said. She tried but could not hold back her tears which flowed down her cheeks. "Betty, don't lose hope too early. As a matter of fact you should be happy because the missionaries are taking good care of him, and most importantly, he is doing very well in school according to the information we have got so far. You have enough time to meet him and explain why you were not able to see him. He is intelligent enough to understand the issues clearly", he consoled her. She raised the helm of her wrapper and wiped away her tears. And suddenly the pillion was ready with his load and that forced him to say a hasty goodbye and moved to the Motorbike. He got the load and the Pillion on the Motorbike and moved away quickly. Biango arrived in Koidu town very late and took the pillion to his desired destination then went in search of additional petrol for the trip to Jaiama the next day. He got some and filled his tank to the brim and went home. Early the next morning, he was already at the place where he had agreed with his client to be. It was only one-way trip hire but he was hopeful that he would not return alone. The client arrived later and the journey began in the early hours of the morning. It was a very cold along the road to Jaiama, as the cool breeze was constantly blowing against his face. His body was protected with a thick sweater which covered him down to his waist. His Jeans trousers covered his legs and tapered into a pair of thick socks which were well secured in a pair of boots. Biango arrived in Jaiama and took the pillion to his destination after which he rode towards Jaiama Secondary School compound. It was too early, and only a handful of students were in the compound. He waited patiently until he spotted Sakayo among a group of students from the Boarding Home. He walked quickly towards him and drew him aside. "Do you know me?" he asked him. "Yes, I do. You are Mr Biango, who brought me back to Kayima when you found me walking towards Yarya without any good reason", he explained with confidence. "Clever boy, you are right I am Biango", he agreed smiling. "How are you doing in school?" he asked. "I am doing fine", he smiled showing his white set of teeth. "Take this envelope. It is from your mother, Betty. I found her yesterday in Kasay-chaindedu, where she is living presently. She wished you well in all your endeavors and promised to pay you a visit any time from now", he explained. "Is she well and strong?" he asked "Yes, she is quite well and strong undoubtedly. She has not changed much", he explained.

Suddenly the School Bell rang for the morning devotional service and Biango said goodbye and went to his Motorbike and rode away to the Jaiama Central Market where he picked up a pillion for Yengema town, and moved away speedily.

Sakayo checked his envelope immediately after the service. He was surprised to find fifty thousand Leones ($6.7) from his poor mother. He knew quite well that she was not comfortable as a single parent, and without support. From that day he decided that he would redouble his efforts in school to be able to qualify in good time in order to take up her responsibility. His chain of thought was broken when a classmate pushed his head and said "Stop day dreaming, the teacher is already in class".

It was time for the Andersons to return home. They disposed of many household utensils to their friends and good neighbors as the time for their departure got closer. They made a trip to Jaiama where they settled Sakayo's other requirements and left him with a good sum of money for his domestic affairs. They spoke to some teachers, especially those who taught him concerning his attitude towards his work. Before they left Jaiama they called Koatambo aside and spoke to him too for a long time concerning Sakayo. Two days after the Andersons left Jaiama, Koatambo walked past him along the Yamba Dormitory, and when he realized that it was him, he gave him a broad smile. That was indeed a strange behavior of somebody everybody feared. His voice and presence always sent shock waves through students. "What could his smile mean?" Sakayo wondered.

It was the month of June; a month which brought showers of rain and caused the environment to be green again. It was also the month which brought abundant fresh mangoes and other fresh fruits to every community member in abundance. With or without money one ate these fruits, especially from the large gardens left behind by Missionaries which had virtually become the Community's property. It was also the month for promotional examinations for Jaiama secondary school, commonly known as J-School. The students were aware of it and behaved cautiously whilst the teachers pressed for it as the final academic exercise that ushered them into the long vacation. For Sakayo, it was also the month for the departure of the Andersons. As he prepared for his examinations his mind went to the Andersons and to his father. "Was he going to continue in the Boarding Home without the Andersons?" he wondered. He could not find answers to the question that kept him awake most often. He concentrated on his studies to maintain his lead in his class. He sat down for long hours and avoided many time-wasting engagements. He initially joined a study group but close to the examinations he broke off and studied alone. By mid-month he got a letter from the Andersons indicating that they had left and encouraged him to work hard. They promised that they would continue to help him. Before this time it was only imaginary that they would go away but now the reality of it was with him. He started to see Kayima and his chores vividly in his imaginations. "Would Nema allow him to go hungry again and to do every chore at home?" he pondered. He tried as much as possible to concentrate on his examinations which were only a few days away. He made sure he went through his own study time table and was satisfied that he would do well. The examinations commenced and within two weeks they were over, making the students joyful once more. Sakayo was convinced he did well. He joined his friends to play football in the mornings and evenings. But they never forgot that the teachers were busy marking their papers. Those who were not quite sure of themselves tried as much as possible to avoid any examinations related discussions. The date for the end of the school year and distribution of results was the 15th July. The Principal, A.J. Sandi (SR.) pressed the teachers to submit all marks on or before the 5th July. He was slow in speech but firm on discipline and the teachers knew it very well. They had no alternative but to concentrate on the marking to ensure that all the marks were available within the given time. On the 10th July the Principal received an envelope with a strange content. It had an air ticket, five hundred US dollars, and a short note addressed to him which read as follows:

Dear Mr. Sandi,

I have enclosed an air ticket and $500 to be given to Sakayo Kebbie's father, to enable Sakayo to travel to the US immediately. I have sent a letter to him directly concerning the trip and what he must do when he arrives in Freetown.

Thanking you in advance for your support in this venture.

My kind regards.

Signed John Anderson.

Sakayo was summoned to the Principal's office the next morning. He did not know why the principal wanted to see him. He was not aware of committing any crime yet he was not comfortable. As he walked up to the office he was nervous and his feet trembled. He tapped on the door and he was asked to enter. "Anything," asked the secretary.

"The Principal has asked me to see him" he said nervously. "What is your name?" asked the secretary again. "Sakayo Kebbie is my name" he said, in a rather shaky voice.

The Secretary went into the Principal's office and announced him. He was asked to come into the office immediately. When he entered he found Koatambo with the Principal and his worries increased. Did he do something wrong in the Boarding Home? He feared.

He stood in front of the two men until he was asked to sit down directly in front of the Principal. "Who are the Andersons to you?" asked Mr. Sandi smiling. "They are my guardians and they have been so kind to me "he said, feeling a little relaxed.

"Who is your father and where is he presently?" Mr. Sandi continued his enquiries.

He is Mr. Entona Kebbie, and currently lives in Kayima, Sandoh Chiefdom" he informed them.

"Do you know anybody who is going to Kayima over the weekend?" he asked again.

"Yes, Mondeh is travelling to Kayima tomorrow. He is a day student staying with the Caulkers". He said with certainty. "Please go and tell him I want him to see me now. I have a message for your father. Thank you very much," he said smiling again. Sakayo came out of the office satisfied that he had not done anything wrong, otherwise the principal would have been annoyed. But he smiled all the time and the mention of the Andersons meant something good for him but they failed to disclose anything. May be the Andersons have sent some good sum of money for his education, and obviously he could not be entrusted with that sum of money. That could be the reason for calling on his father to come immediately. Anyway, he waited to see what would happen and he kept everything as a secret to himself. Three days later Entona got a letter from Mr. Anderson and a message from the Principal. He came home early to prepare for the journey to Jaiama. But first of all, he had to convince Nema that it was a worthwhile journey and he spoke to her in confidence.

"I have received an urgent message from Sakayo's Principal urging me to be in Jaiama immediately" he explained to her. "Is he sick or has he done something bad?" she asked anxiously. "No, the message was, come to Jaiama now concerning your son Sakayo", he explained. "Please don't spend all your money on him. We hope to have my own children here to take care of," she added. Entona avoided any confrontation on the issue by making no comments. The next day he left for Jaiama.

He arrived there in time to see the Principal late in the afternoon. He took Sakayo along to see the Principal at his residence. They arrived there and tapped on the door twice. The main door opened and he appeared and received them warmly. "Welcome", he said and invited them to sit with him in his parlor. They discussed many other issues, at the end of which he brought out the ticket and money and handed them over to him. "Make sure you take this boy to Freetown immediately. The date of his flight is Thursday, which is barely two days away. Try to ensure that he makes good use of this opportunity" he said and then turned to Sakayo "Young man, go and study and try to come back home to help your people. I went to England to study but returned home after my studies, and now I am happy helping my people". He explained. Sakayo nodded his head in support of his request. He then brought out his results and other relevant documents for his journey. He praised him for leading his class in the final examinations. They travelled to Koidu town that same evening so that they could catch the early morning bus to Freetown. They found a lodge close to the bus park and got up very early the next morning to occupy the first and second seats of the bus.

Chapter Seven

The Journey

The journey to Freetown was long but it was good for Sakayo. He saw many big towns which his teachers had talked about often in their lessons. He wanted to know these towns so that when they were discussed in the lessons he would be one of those who would proudly say "I know them all." Sometimes he felt embarrassed when he was asked whether he had been to Makeni or to Bo but unfortunately he had not been to either of them.

As a matter of fact he did not know any big town apart from Koidu town and he admired some of his classmates who had been to most of the big towns. He wondered how they did it. One day he asked a pupil who claimed he had been to many big towns to explain how he had done it. It was at that point he knew that the boy's father's job moved them from one town to other every two years. He wished his father had such a job which took him to various towns around the country. The bus had made significant progress despite the bad road network. They were in Magburaka and he had to stand up to have a clear view of the town. He liked standing up in the bus not only to have a better view but to enjoy the cool breeze that blew through the window close to his seat. He continued checking on the big towns until they arrived in Freetown.

Walking close by his father they moved quickly across the street to avoid over speeding cars and vehicles. They walked into an office and his father turned around and whispered to him "This is British Airways". He concentrated on the beauty of the office whilst his father handed over the ticket to a lady he had been speaking to since they entered the office.

The ticket was processed and he was told the journey was on Friday at 10 a. m. at the Lungi International Airport. He was asked to bring Sakayo to the office by 7 a.m. that day to be on board the first Ferry to Lungi. They moved out of the office and went to the International Hotel at Rawdon Street where they ate and stayed for the two nights they were in Freetown. Sakayo wanted to see more of Freetown but he had very limited time and he had to be by his father's side all the time because he did not know the city, and the crowd along the streets was big enough for him to get in and be lost immediately. He had heard stories of children who got lost because they could not find their way back home when they went for a walk without their parents. By 8 am on Thursday morning they were at Cline Town to receive the yellow card and other medical travelling documents. They waited until it was Sakayo's turn to be attended to. He went into the office and came out later with all the documents that he needed for the trip. While he was in the office, Entona had already located a restaurant nearby where they took breakfast and later boarded a taxi back to the International Hotel in good time. Late in the evening they walked to the National Stadium for sight seeing. Sakayo was amazed to see the giant structure and fortunately for them a match was playing between members of the same football club as part of their daily drill. Father and son watched the match to its end and enjoyed it. It ended in a goalless draw but the competition was not as keen as between rival teams. At the end of the match they walked back to the Hotel and got ready for the trip to Lungi. Early the next morning they were at

British Airways where they boarded a bus to Lungi. It was an amazing trip again for Sakayo, especially the ferry crossing trip to Lungi. He came out of the bus when it safely entered the ferry and parked. He could not believe that the ferry could take so many vehicles apart from theirs and did not show any sign of sinking. He felt that the load was too much for the Ferry. Anyway, it carried them across safely to the other side. They arrived at Lungi International Airport and occupied a room over-looking a vast field. The room was full of people with their luggage besides them and waiting patiently for the arrival of the Airplane which was to leave Lungi that morning. It was late according to passengers who kept looking at their wrist watches from time to time. He had a small travelling bag and a purse containing the ticket and other documents relating to the journey. Within an hour there was a noise in the air and when he looked up he saw an object like a big bird whose wings were not flapping. As the noise became louder the object turned out to be the Airplane everybody was waiting for. He had heard and seen Airplanes in the air before but that particular one was very big and very noisy. It came past by the building where they were sitting and he held unto his father's arm for fear that he might fall down. Within the next half hour the room emptied into a single file which moved towards an office and checking in commenced in earnest. The process was fast because Sakayo had moved close to the office which saw everyone before going out to the Airplane, was heading for Califonia in the US

Entona came close to him and spoke to him passionately. "Please, when you are out there pay attention to your work and consider the Andersons as your parents. Don't be distracted by your peers and stay

93

out of all forms of crime. And consider returning home when you are appropriately qualified so that you can help your people," he advised as he moved away into the office. A few seconds later he came out and waved at Entona and walked out of the building into the open space where the Airplane was waiting. A few minutes later it taxied and flew away.

Entona arrived in Kayima after a week. His journey was a successful one because he was on time for all the engagements and at the end of it all Sakayo was able to travel abroad. This made him a proud and hopeful father. He could not keep the secret to himself because his son's departure made him more important in the society. He therefore contacted his club members and gave them the news during the evening entertainment session at his club.

From the club he arrived back home at night and found Nema in a bad mood and tried to engage her tactically to avoid any quarrels. "How is your son doing in school? Did he cause some havoc in school?" She asked rather provocatively. "No, on the contrary he has done extremely well by leading his class," he replied confidently. "So, how much money did you spend on him this time? I hope you are saving some money so that when I bear children there would be enough money for their use," she said angrily. "Look, stop fooling about, Sakayo has got good friends, and as I speak to you now, he is in the United States of America," he informed her. "That does not mean anything to me because I am going to have my own children anyway. I observe that you are joyful because you cannot take care of your own son. Instead you have shifted that responsibility to the Missionaries whom you don't quite know. When are you going to take up your own responsibility? She exploded with anger.

Entona looked on sheepishly as Nema lambasted him. He was tired and needed an uninterrupted sleep. He located the Thermos flask and poured out some hot water into a cup to which he added some sugar and some cocoa powder to facilitate an early sleep. He gulped the mixture and went to bed.

Sakayo arrived in California and was once more well received by the Andersons. A lot of work had been done in the home of the Andersons to accommodate him. On his arrival, he found that Skyline High School had already been arranged for him. It was there he was assessed and placed in fifth grade. The school was not too far away from his residential area, but it was not a walking distance. He was taken to school every morning by Mrs. Anderson for a long time until he understood the public transport system, after which he went to school by himself. In school he thought he would be the only African in his class but on the contrary there were five others besides him. Surprisingly however, they did not come close to him. Instead it was the white guys that befriended him and asked him a lot of questions about his country and parents. But with time, all of them in class got used to each other, played games together and called each other by the first name. He found that learning in the US was easy because there were up to date books on every subject and other necessary material for learning, and the teachers were well off and more committed to the work. If there was something he did not understand he would meet the teacher concerned and explain his problems. The teachers took their time to explain what he did not understand. He loved asking questions where

95

there were doubts in his notes or in some explanations in any subject. The teachers were happy that he was brave and challenged whatever he did not understand. By the time he was in grade six he became well known in the class, particularly for Mathematics. He was not on top of the class but he was a force to reckon with. The teachers as well as classmates were quite aware of his ability in all subjects and demonstrated a high spirit of competition. At home he was overwhelmed by the wonders of television. He enjoyed the programs so much that there was a tendency for him to overdo things. But the Andersons were smart to notice his concentration on the TV and cautioned him about the consequences of viewing all the programs. He was therefore advised to be very selective in choosing his programs and ensured that the programs began when he had completed his school assignments. He had a room to himself with all sorts of clothing according to the weather. He loved his new environment very much with its fantastic buildings, attractive vehicles and the broad motors ways. When he had settled in school Mr. Anderson tried and got Entona on the phone and gave father and son the opportunity to talk. They had a long discussion in which Sakayo catalogued his experiences in the US, especially the type of school he attended and the striking differences between Jaiama Secondary School and Skyline High School.

For the first time he was bold enough to ask about his mother but his father was not able to say something concrete about her, but he promised to update him the next time they had such an opportunity. The discussion ended well but Entona was a bit embarrassed by his shocking question to which he could not provide the required answers. He however encouraged him to endeavor to talk to him from time to time so that he could gather information on Betty. For the first time he felt guilty about the manner in which she got separated from him.

At home he understood the Andersons very well when they spoke to him in English but other speakers were too fast for him. He recalled that when he stayed with them for the first time in Koidu town, he had some difficulty understanding what they said to him. They had to repeat or speak slowly so that he could understand what they wanted him to know. But over time he got over it and tried as much as possible to speak up boldly, ignoring any grammatical errors. And with time he was able to catch up. At home he was most of the time by himself and was strictly instructed not to go out of the house without Permission. He was told that there were people who tried as much as possible to harm children or to kidnap and take them to unknown hideouts. He noticed for himself that when children played outdoors, they were always under supervision and not allowed to be alone. He wished he had somebody of his age at home so that they could work and play together. He recalled that when he was in Kayima or in Jaiama he went to visit his friends without any supervision. When he came to the US he found that the only child of the Andersons had graduated from university quite a long time ago. He got married and took up a job in another State and had never come back to see his parents since he arrived. But he called them often and it was during one of those calls that his father made the introduction and allowed them to talk. They spoke for a short time and he was concerned about his studies and what he would like to do in the future. The son had virtually the same concern for Sakayo as his father had for him.

Since his arrival in the US, life had been good and his school work had been smooth and without any problems. He did not realize that time had moved so fast and that he had been transformed physically. One morning he looked at himself in the mirror and realized that he had grown twice his original size and his height had increased. He was in the eleventh grade and busy preparing for the final examinations at the end of the twelfth grade. He had already applied to the Department of Mechanical Engineering at the famous Hastings College where some of his friends wanted to attend as well. At home in the US he had a whole lot of new games just like in his school. He loved all the new games but he had a passion for football where he was rated very high both by his colleagues and the games master of the School. He took the twelfth grade final examinations a year later and passed with good grades which made his admission at Hastings College very easy. He had made some calls to his father when he got his own cell phone but most often the calls did not go through because he was out of coverage and that pained him most. He was furious one day when he had a missed call from Betty and tried to call back but the line was cracking so badly that all he heard was "I am well and praying for your success" and the line went mute. Further attempts to reach her were futile and for a long time she did not call until quite recently. Although the call was brief because he was ready to go to class, they were able to discuss issues like when would he complete his studies and when would he come back home.

The next academic year found him at Hastings College. He was not surprised to find that some of his former classmates were in class with him and offering the same subjects. And that made life for him much easier because he was already in a group of white folks who were working with him closely. At every level of his work he was a forced to reckon with and he was so simple that most members of the class liked him. His academic foundation was solid and that helped him to move from first year to the fourth year without any problems that might cause him to repeat a class and prolong his years at the College. But the fourth year proved different from the other academic years. He had to do internship with a company of his choice and that was to take about three months. He chose a mining company not far away from the College and he happened to be the only one from his College. He approached the internship with extra zeal when it was time for it. He articulated well and knew exactly what was required of him as an intern. He loved the work that was assigned to him and discharged his duties fully. Sometimes the permanent staff took him as one of them mistakenly because he worked like any of them.

At the end of three months he returned to College with a document from the company indicating a very good performance during the Internship. And that piece of recommendation formed part of his final assessment for the degree course, and thereafter he took the final examinations and passed with flying colors. He qualified as a mechanical engineer after nearly five years of serious academic work. He was tempted to stay in the US because the opportunities that he looked for were all present there but he was conscious about the promise to his parents that he would return home and help them and make a meaningful contributions to the community and to his mother in Particular. The thought of returning home to help his people lingered in his mind throughout his stay in the US. But at the same time he knew quite well that coming back home was like stepping out in the dark. He did not know the job market back home and the conditions of service for employees. But he valued his promise more than anything he stood to gain in the US. The Andersons were happy to hear that he had decided to return home to help his people. They too encouraged him to do so whenever he was ready. They advised him to work for at most one year to secure some basic necessities of life, especially articles that were found to be abnormally expensive in his country. He thought over it and agreed to stay for one year to buy a car, a generator and other items that he had put as priority. He felt his parents needed special gifts and Kaye too needed some good gifts. Based on his new demands he picked up a job in a company where his salary and other conditions of service were good. He felt good working in the company which afforded him the opportunity to exercise the skills that he learnt in college. Each month he bought some items in accordance with his scale of preference and saved some amount. Within one year he bought most of the items that he needed and shipped them, making sure that he would have arrived in Sierra Leone before the ship's arrival.

He tendered his letter of resignation to the managing director of the company as a first step to leave the US. His friends were not happy with his decision to return home almost immediately after graduation but he was able to convince them that he had made a promise to his parents that he would return home to help them and to locate his mother who was a single parent and support her for the rest of her life. At his farewell party organized by the Andersons a week later, he praised them for taking care of him throughout the duration of his studies. He informed the gathering further that he was picked up by the Andersons in Kayima where he attended school under difficult circumstances and was finally brought over to the land of opportunities. He assured the gathering that he would always maintain a link with them no matter where he might be and ensure that the bond of friendship continued to exist always. To his school mates, college mates and friends, he said bravo for a well cultivated friendship. He assured them that their memories would stay with him forever. Before the party came to a close, Mrs. Anderson presented him a brown envelope as a gift, after which his friends sang a farewell song which moved the whole gathering. The song actually climaxed the occasion and it remained in his mind for a long time.

Chapter Eight

A Promise Fulfilled

The next morning the Andersons and a handful of friends, in two separate cars, accompanied him to the airport. Before he checked in, he turned solemnly and waved frantically at his friends who had formed a small group outside the waiting room. They too waved back with the same zeal and watched him until he disappeared into the Airplane. The Airplane plane transited in Ghana before arriving at Lungi International Airport in Freetown, Sierra Leone where all the passengers disembarked and went into the arrival lounge. There they waited patiently for the customs and immigration officers. At the Lungi International Airport, Sakayo went through all of the formalities and was finally at the desk of the Immigration officer. He produced his passport which the officer examined with some curiosity. "Are you a Sierra Leonean?" asked the officer. "Yes I am." He said. "Where is your home town?" asked the officer again, still looking into his passport. "My home town is Kayima, Sandoh chiefdom, Kono District", he informed him. "Welcome back home", said the officer who placed his hand in his and shook it firmly. He then returned his passport and continued his interrogation. "Which primary school did you attend?" he asked in a rather cordial manner. "I attended the United Methodist Church School, Kayima", he explained. "My name is Kaye. Does that ring a bell?" he asked with anxiety in his voice.

"Yes, it does. I had a friend with the same name. He was a good guy and we liked each other so much." He narrated, anxious to know the identity of the officer. "Ok, listen to me. Think of any number. Multiply it by fifty, and divide the product by the number you first thought of, and then you will know who I am", Kaye directed. Sakayo jumped at him and hugged him saying "You are undoubtedly my friend Kaye." "Yes, I am and pleased that you are back home and looking good", he assured him. Sakayo took his telephone number and home address because they did not have enough time to say all that they wanted to say to each other as Kaye was on duty with clients waiting on him. Before he left Kaye's desk, Sakayo asked him whether he could hire a taxi to Freetown. Kaye turned around and asked a gentleman standing by his office to take him to Lanso, the taxi driver. They hastily said goodbye to each other and the gentleman led him away to the car park where they found Lanso in the car and introduced Sakayo to him. He then walked back to the office to continue his work. Sakayo loaded his luggage into the car, after agreeing on the fare to his destination. He did not know anybody in Freetown but he remembered the International Hotel at Rawdon Street. Lanso knew the hotel very well and was prepared to take him there. He sped through the distance to the Ferry Terminal to catch up with the Ferry. He arrived there in time and drove into it and occupied a position under the guidance of the ferry's security officers. Sakayo and Lanso found themselves in the ferry's restaurant where the two men had food and drinks while the Ferry moved rather slowly across River Rokel to Freetown. Sakayo was tired and went back to the car where he fell asleep a few minutes later. When he woke up, the car was already out of the ferry, making its way up to Upgun Roundabout. When they arrived at the International Hotel, he saw the receptionist who chatted with him for some time and then sent him over to the accountant. At the accountant's he paid for food and lodging for a number of days. He was shown his room and given a single key to the room. Lanso moved quickly between the car and the Hotel bringing along his luggage. At the end of the exercise Sakayo paid him off and added a bonus for his extra effort and time.

A few days after his arrival he checked his notebook for the addresses of the companies where he had applied for work while he was in America. He found the address and went in search of them across the city. He found them and gave them his contact addresses in Freetown. Late in the afternoon that same day, he went to a Telecenter and made a call to Kaye who had already returned to Freetown. They had a long telephone conversation on various issues. At the end of it all, they agreed on a meeting to be held at his Hotel. The next day Kaye arrived at the hotel on time and he received him at the gate with joy. Their discussions started with Kaye giving a brief history about his life after he had left Kayima. He told him the schools he attended, and explained in detail his experiences before he got the job at the Immigrations Department. He informed him that two years later he brought along his younger sister Kumba Kaye to Freetown. She attended Koidu Girl's Secondary School up to the forth form and stayed in the Boarding Home until she made a passionate appeal to him to continue her schooling in Freetown due to the falling education standards in Kono District. Sakayo looked on with much interest as he narrated his story which was challenging but well managed in-order to gain a successful career. When it was Sakayo's turn to narrate his story, he began with his flight to America. He explained how it was so fearful that he forced himself to sleep or pretended to be asleep to hide his fear. In fact, he closed his eyes for most of time until he fell asleep. He explained that when he woke up he found a tray of food and drinks resting on the arm of his chair and a lady encouraging him to choose what he wanted to eat. He did not eat enough food as he did not know where the Rest Room was and in fact, he did not want to bother himself asking for it. He explained that when he arrived in America the reception was very good but he found virtually everything very strange indeed. The way of talking, walking and even the food that was available. He told him that he coped with life at home, in school and in the university. To illustrate his success, he brought out his degree certificate in Mechanical Engineering which his friend read over and over, shook his hand for a brilliant performance and handed it back to him. They had food and drinks together and sat there for many hours discussing many issues relating to their childhood. When Sakayo realized that it was getting late, he went into his room and brought two shirts, a wrist watch and two pairs of leather shoes all of which happened to be Kaye's correct size. Kaye thanked him for being so kind to him and was happy that time had not killed their well cultivated friendship. He assured him of his fullest co-operation always.

Then Sakayo informed him about the challenge of identifying a flat to rent and locating his mother and bringing her to Freetown. Kaye took up both responsibilities. He promised that within a week he would have got somewhere as far the flat was concerned. With respect to locating his mother, he assured him that his cousin would be an appropriate person to run that errand. Sakayo was so impressed with him that he provided him enough money to take care of his transportation whilst searching for the flat.

Kaye was familiar with the city. He decided that he would concentrate on Brookfields and if he did not succeed there he would move to Congo Cross. He did not want to disappoint his friend so he made up his mind to commence the search the next day with all seriousness. Very early the next day he was out on the streets of Brookfields. He had the opportunity to talk to many landlords but they told him there was no vacancy. He did not give up but continued on a different street until he got a piece of information relating to a flat at Bass Street. When he arrived there he was advised to see the agent at 105 Wellington Street at 2pm the next day. He took his time to speak to the landlord whose address was given to him by somebody in the neighborhood who believed that talking directly to the landlord himself would be helpful. When he met him he did not mince his words concerning the flat. "It is gone. But everything will depend on how many years you are prepared to pay for, at the rate of $4000 per annum" he told him. He thought about it for a moment and then asked him to give him up to the next day. At the end of that meeting he went back to Sakayo and shared with him the piece of information. They discussed and came to the conclusion that it was worth the price because they wanted that part of the city at all cost. They initially agreed on two years but if the landlord pressed for more years they would pay for three years, taking into consideration too that he was expecting his mother to join him. The next day the two of them went to see the landlord. They were desperate for a flat in an ideal location and Kaye had already decided it was. They found him and explained what they had decided. "Look here friends, if you can pay for three years the flat is yours. Somebody has paid but I will change my decision once there is agreement on three years", he said. The young men looked at each other and agreed to pay for three years and the landlord went into his room and came out with a note on his letterhead to a Mr. Gilpen, who happened to be his lawyer. "Make sure you see him today" he told them. They boarded a taxi to Wellington Street but found out that Mr Gilpin was still in court. They handed the letter over to the secretary and decided to wait. Mr. Gilpen arrived at his office an hour later and found the two men waiting for him. The secretary asked them to see him when he had read the note from his client, the landlord. They went into his office, which was rather a very small room with two chairs for the clients and many law books neatly organized on the tables which completely surrounded him. He asked them to sit down whilst he continued writing on a piece of paper on his table. After some minutes he put the paper aside and concentrated on them. "Are you here in connection with the flat at Bass Street?" he asked quickly. He had limited time as he had to represent another client in court in the next hour. "Yes" said Sakayo. "Are you ready with the money for three years?" he asked again looking at his watch. "Yes I am" said Sakayo, choosing his words in such a way to avoid making any mistakes. "Right, come up with the money and the secretary will issue the receipt to you immediately" he assured them. Sakayo took out the money from his handbag and Kaye recounted it before handling it over to Mr. Gilpen. "Who is the tenant, his name and address please?" requested Mr. Gilpen. "My name is Sakayo Kebbie, Kayima town, Sandoh Chiefdom" he said. Mr. Gilpen brought out an agreement which he handed over to him to read and sign if he found it appropriate and passed over to his secretary the details for the preparation of the receipt.

Within a short time the receipt was ready and the agreement was signed and witnessed by Kaye. The keys to the flat at 200Y Bass Street were handed over to the witness who then handed them over to Sakayo the tenant. Sakayo and Kaye went in haste to look at the flat from the inside. First of all, it was fenced and had a car park. They opened each room and examined its facilities. At the end of the day they were satisfied that it was indeed a good flat with modern facilities. Two days later Sakayo's container arrived at the Deep Water Quay and he was notified in good time. He discussed with Kaye and at once they both went there. They hired a Clearing and Forwarding Agent who filled and filed the forms at the appropriate offices. It was nearly after two days that they were able to clear it and move it to his new address. They engaged some young men in the area who helped transport the items from the container into the house under the watchful eyes of the two men and for a fee which was negotiated and agreed by both parties. It was not an easy task but with Kaye on his side, they had a neatly arranged flat. That same night he moved into the flat even though there was still some work to be done because some items were still not in their proper places. By and large, he was satisfied he had got a decent home in a neighborhood which was not densely populated and relatively quiet. In the evening he called the Andersons and briefed them about the challenges that he had ahead of him and the successful gains that he had made. They were very happy to hear from him and congratulated him for his new job.

A week later Kaye and his cousin Simeon come to see Sakayo in connection with the search for his mother. He was more than prepared to receive Simeon, the person who he was told knew the terrain well enough and who had the necessary information to accomplish the assignment. It was a simple assignment to locate his mother, Betty. All the pieces of information indicated that she was within the borders of Kono District. But if she went outside Kono then Simeon may not track her down. Sakayo spoke to him for a long time after which he gave him sufficient money to take him anywhere in Kono District. He also gave him some guidance which he noted down in a notebook and got ready for the trip. He was particularly advised to go to a village called Kasay-Chaindedu where she was last seen. Simeon bought a flash light and some candles and placed them in his handbag before setting out on the journey. He went to the lorry park and boarded an early bus to Koidu town. He checked his pockets and handbag to ensure that his money and articles were intact. He knew he was in a den of pick pockets and thieves. The articles in the handbag were correct and the money had the seal which he had put on it. He felt good after the exercise and bought a few more items through the window of the bus from hawkers who were in the park. Before the bus left, he contemplated on the journey ahead of him and Betty's whereabouts. He knew that to locate her was a huge challenge but he was determined not to fail. As a result he made some enquiries in the bus about Kasay-chaindedu and he got some useful pieces of information.

In Freetown Sakayo was positive that Betty was alive and living with some relative somewhere. But still some negative thoughts flashed through his mind each time he thought about her. If Betty went outside Kono District the possibility to locate her was slim and this thought caused pain in his head and reversed all the good plans that he had for her. But he trusted Simeon very much and hoped that he would be successful in locating her where she stayed after she left Kayima.

One evening Sakayo had his dinner in the Hotel. He was alone at his residence and so did not intend to stay for long. He ate his food almost in haste and drank a pint of Fanta. He called for his bill and the waitress gave him the bill and a letter. "We received this letter for you this morning sir" she said. "Thank you", he replied and then paid his bill and gave her back his change as a tip. He checked the letter roundabout for any marks or writings that may give an idea about the sender but there was absolutely nothing. He took his time to open it partially from one edge. He got it barely opened and drew the letter out and read it through quickly. It was from Kubic Hire International (KHI), one of the companies he had applied to for a job. It was a company with generators, bailing machines and Earth moving machines for sale and on hire. He left the Hotel and went home feeling good, although he had not analyzed the letter fully. He arrived home and sat down immediately to read and understand the contents of the letter. He found he had barely two days to appear for an interview and was required to produce his certificates that he claimed he had. Additionally, he had to prove he had got enough practical experience in the field. He was not afraid because he was confident about his work experience in the US.

Betty arrived in Samadu a day before Simeon arrived in Kasay-chaindedu. She went to see relatives and did not say exactly when she would return as she was on holidays.

She went to see her relatives after two years with some gifts because they knew that she was a teacher. She brought some Gara clothes for her aunt and two pairs of shoes for her uncle. Additionally, she brought some money, without which nothing worked well enough. Her relatives were very happy about her visit and encouraged her to continue visiting them.

Simeon was advised to wait on the belief that she normally would not stay long and he waited for two days but she had not come. His anxiety increased with every passing second and he regretted why he had not walked to Samadu in the first place. He made up his mind to give her another day, after which he would go there despite the long distance.

Sakayo waited patiently to be interviewed. There were five other young men with him in the room prepared for the interview but he could not tell whether they were there for the same purpose. But that became clearer when a lady came in and read out the names of the candidates to be interviewed. He was the third person to be called into the room where the interviews began. He entered, presented his documents and remained standing until he was asked to sit down. Thereafter he was asked a series of questions relating to the job, his work experience and his relationship with his workmates and senior cadre of the organization in which he worked. He felt he gave appropriate answers to most of the questions. But one question that kept him uneasy was the one which demanded an explanation for leaving a job in the US to compete for a lesser paid one in Sierra Leone. But for that too he did his best but the question kept coming up. "Why did you resign from a well-paid job in America to compete for one with a lesser pay out here?" asked one of the panelists. "I resigned to fulfill a promise to my parents, that is, to return home after my studies in order to help them", he informed the panelist. At the end of the Interview he received his documents and left the room feeling confident

Another day had come and passed and Betty had still not returned. Simeon became impatient and made up his mind to walk to Samadu. He said goodbye to his hosts and left after he had received guidance on the footpath and the crossroads. He was zealous and determined to return to Kasay-Chaindedu the same day. He walked so fast that he appeared to be running. After a long walk he came to a high hill and he had been told in advance that after the hill was a river. He was thirsty and decided to quench his thirst there. The hill was indeed high and he needed some zeal to climb it. He rested for some time and then moved up the hill like walking on a flat land, and within a short time he was on top of it. He sweated all over his body and sat down on a rock to cool down. Whilst he was there his attention was drawn to somebody coming in the opposite direction. He got ready and stood up and saw a woman walking to towards the hill. He watched further whether the description of Betty matched with that of the woman who had come closer. He could not confirm because she was still not very close. His curiosity could no longer allow him to wait but ran down the hill quickly and moved towards the woman. "Good morning madam. Are you Betty, Sakayo's mother?" he asked, trying to control his breathing. The woman stood still for some time. Her eyes lit up and she observed the man before her from head to foot. Many things ran through her mind that kept her speechless. Then suddenly she came to herself and saw the need to reply. "Yes I am. Is anything wrong with him?" she asked with a rattle and shaky voice. "He is well, and he is the one who sent me to take you to Freetown" explained Simeon. "Are you sure he is alive?" she again asked, still in doubt. "He is undoubtedly alive. He returned from America recently and he is presently in Freetown", explained Simeon. Betty started to have confidence because she was told that he would return to home any time. They walked back to Kasay-chaindedu almost in complete silence. Betty felt that if Sakayo was in danger the message could be the same. But she believed in her prayers concerning him. They arrived home and she found the message to be the same. The relatives out there convinced her to travel the next day and she was comfortable with the date. She cleaned up her travelling bag and put into it the few items she had.

Sakayo received a letter from KHI barely two days after the interview. He took the letter to his bedroom and prayed before opening it. He jumped up and shouted "Praise be to God". He was offered the Job. He called Kaye on the phone and explained that he had got a job with KHI, a company which Kaye knew very well. After talking to him, he drove to KHI and completed the documentation that was required of him, in accordance with the letter of appointment. He was asked to commence work two days after he had completed the documentation process.

Betty and Simeon took off early the next morning. Betty was now convinced that Simeon was not deceiving her because the little things he knew about Sakayo he explained clearly without any doubt and with confidence. "Who is his cook?" she asked further. "When he arrived from America, he lodged in the International Hotel from where he also got his meals", he explained. Betty was full of suspicion at the beginning of the journey but the discussions helped her further to conclude that he was not lying because he had seen some consistency in the answers to the many questions that were posed to him over the short period of time that they had been together. They boarded a vehicle to Freetown when they arrived at the highway. They spent the whole day travelling and before sunset they were in Freetown. They hired a taxi which took them across the city to 200Y Bass Street. As the taxi hooted at the gate, Sakayo came out and embraced Betty so warmly that both mother and child shed tears. What had happened to Betty was like a dream. She did not believe at any moment that she would ever come to Freetown especially on a call from her son, Sakayo. But the reality was that she was in Freetown despite all the challenges that she had in her life. Sakayo bought her a lot of dresses, a suitcase and many other miscellaneous items that completely changed her physical appearance. He sent her to Connaught Hospital for proper medical check-up and because she did not know the city, Simeon was asked to accompany her to the Hospital and see her through the various processes. They boarded a taxi to the Hospital and contacted the doctor in charge of the outpatient. She went through various tests and waited patiently in the waiting room for the results. It was whilst she and Simeon were waiting that a group of women entered the room demanding applications forms to be trained as nurses. Betty showed some interest in the course because she wanted to be a nurse before she dropped out of School. She realized she could opt for nursing because she was qualified according to her WASSSCE results. Simeon moved quickly to see the officer in charge and got the forms free of charge. She was happy to complete the forms there and then and presented them to the appropriate authority before the result of her medical tests came out. Only one result showed that she had hookworms for which a prescription form was given. They returned home and broke the news about her ambition to be trained as a nurse at Connaught Hospital. The news made Sakayo happy and moved him to secure all that she required for her studies, including an appropriate financial support. He bought the prescribed drugs and she commenced her treatment immediately. The next day she gathered some books and began to read them with the hope of updating her knowledge and improving her reading skills. Within two weeks she was advised that the course would commence the following Monday and that she would receive a kit which would be paid for at the end of the course which was expected to last for three years. Success in the first examination would qualify a nurse to be transferred to the provincial hospitals, where there was an acute shortage of nurses and Betty was looking forward to working in Koidu town. Sakayo bought some drinks and entertained his mother, Kaye and Simeon who had contributed immensely for locating her and helping her to take advantage of the training programme. They drank and ate together until it was late. Before the two men left, Sakayo gave Simeon some money for his marvelous job of locating his mother and for being helpful and kind to the entire family. Simeon appreciated it very much and showed Kaye the contents of the envelope. Both of them thanked Sakayo for being reasonable and kind. Within a few days he employed a cleaner who also helped Betty to prepare the meals. Mother and son lived together for one week enjoying the account of each other's life whilst they were separated for a long period of time. The following Monday found her quite ready for the course. Sakayo took her to the hospital every morning and taught her the road network from Brookfields to Connaught; where to wait for buses, Poda Podas and taxis and how much to pay in each case. He did that in case he failed to take her due to either mechanical or other problems beyond his control. She began the course with zeal, trying to prove to her son that dropping out of School did not mean that she was stupid. She worked hard from day one and ensured that she remained on the course because she had the requisite foundation from her private studies at home. She was proud of her new profession and became anxious to return home after her graduation to help her community.

When she was fully established on her course Sakayo sent a letter to Entona in addition to the telephone calls he made on his arrival. He explained that he was back from America as a qualified mechanical engineer, and that he had picked up a job in Freetown. He told him that he would be paying him a visit on Saturday the 3rd June, which was on a weekend, and at the end of the letter he indicated that he would be coming with his mother Betty and his friend Kaye. A day before the journey to Kayima, Betty and Sakayo spent many hours in the parlor discussing some of the expected outcomes of the journey. And at the end of their discussion, he asked his mother a question that lingered in his mind from his youth.

"Mother, why did you leave my father's house when I was too young?" "Thank you very much" Betty responded. "I was expecting this question since I came here, and I am happy you have asked me to explain. This is an indication that you have grown up physically and you have become a matured man. I lost my position as a wife when your father got another wife. I tried but failed to convince him to reverse his decision but he refused. Then I asked him to let him allow me to take you along but that request too he refused. You may want to know why I did not pair up with the new wife for your sake. Let me tell you plainly that I did not have the inner strength to do so", she explained. "What do you think about him now?" Sakayo asked again. "I have forgiven both of them, that is, Entona and Nema. I believe that what God wanted me to have out of the relationship is your success, and indeed you have been blessed. I am thankful to God for everything that has happened to you. And from today, Know that Nema's only daughter is your only sister and you must support her wherever the opportunity exists" she advised. "Thank you very much for the details and good night", Sakayo said and went to his bedroom.

Entona received the letter with joy but was surprised to hear that Betty was in Freetown. He went about spreading the news, especially to his club members and the news was everywhere in the town and everybody looked forward to seeing the visitors. Even the neighboring villages had heard the news that Sakayo, Entona's son was back from America and was paying a visit to his relatives and they too were hopeful to see him. Entona was still waiting for Nema's reaction to Sakayo's visit. When she received the news she did not utter a word. She went into her room and remained there for a

117

long time and when she came out she feigned as if nothing had happened. She continued plaiting the hair of her only daughter Mary who was always by her side. Entona did not disclose the entire content of the letter to anybody because Betty was coming with Sakayo. He kept it secret because he could not tell how Nema would react to it. Already she had shown no interest in Sakayo's visit. What if he had disclosed that Betty was on the trip? He treated the whole affair casually, hoping that something would happen to prevent any quarrels at home. But as the days went by, he started to see the seriousness of having Betty and Nema under the same roof. It was only at the point in time that he saw the need to secure another lodge for the visitors but besides that he realized that there were gaps in the whole arrangement. As a result he decided to consult Chief Soui Nampanneh Songowa who listened to his story attentively and then at the end he laughed and shook his head with disgust and commented on the issue thus; "There is a parable which says that when you are looking for some medicine for healing sores, you must look for somebody with the biggest scar," he said and continued laughing. "Have you come to me for a solution to your marital problem because I have many wives? Yes indeed, I have many wives but they are obedient and under my control. On the contrary, you have a single wife but she sits right on your head. Anyway, what exactly do you want?" he asked. "Accommodation for the visitors" he told him. "Call me Fanta," he said to him and within a few minutes Fanta, one of his wives came and bowed down before him. "I want you to lodge Entona's visitors in my second house. You will cook and attend to them whilst they are here. Work with Entona on the details of what is required", he ordered. Entona went back home and found Nema waiting. "How far has the news gone?" she asked. "What news? He replied." "The news about your son's coming. You are not even sure whether he is actually coming but you have propagated the news everywhere. What if he does not come? You will be considered a liar. Mark what I am saying to you", she elaborated.

Sakayo had already bought the items required for the journey. They included foodstuff, clothes, books, pens and pencils and he had prepared envelopes too for his father and other close relatives. On the 3rd June Kaye moved over to Sakayo early in the morning and helped him arrange the luggage in the car. They ate and took some food along for lunch and possibly for dinner. They took off in the early hours of the morning. The distance was long to Kayima and the road was in a bad shape but with a four wheel drive Jeep, they were able to cover a reasonable ground in good time. They had already gone past Makeni and Magburaka and were moving towards Matotoka, where passengers normally had lunch and some rest. When they arrived at Matotoka they stopped and ate some of the food they brought along. They also bought some fresh fruits. Sakayo was reminded of his days in Kayima when he saw some fresh wild fruits on sale. He recalled how he desperately climbed trees to have some fruits in order to survive. Betty realized that he was thinking too deeply and broke his chain of thought by asking, "What is the matter?" "I am reflecting on my past and trying to figure out what Kayima would look like;" he said trying to avoid making any references. "Don't worry; you will be there very soon", she said. They arrived in Yengema and then drove towards

Yormadu on a pretty bad road. Everybody was fully awake as the car rocked left and right down Tegbadu hill and then surged forward where the road was good. They passed through Baudu and arrived in Kayima at dusk, and parked the car in front of Entona's house. Entona came out followed by Mary his daughter. And one after another the neighbors came out and formed a crowd with the three in the middle. They did not shake hands inorder to comply with the emergency Ebola regulations but instead put their hands on their chests to symbolize hand shaking and tried to talk to each one that came to greet them. Sakayo was not happy about his father's appearance. He was very thin and he coughed perpetually. He looked at him quickly from head to toe and concluded that he needed medical attention. Nema was completely absent from the crowd. She stayed in her room and observed what went on outside the house through the window from where nobody could see her. Initially she thought the lady in the car was Sakayo's wife but on close examination she turned out to be Betty, Sakayo's mother and that made a big difference to her. She was shocked that she was part of the trip and amazed how well dressed and good looking she was. She actually wanted to come out to greet them but some force held her back. And besides, the other issue was why did Entona hide the news of Betty's coming from her? She felt there was a plot behind his behavior which she needed to investigate. She was also constrained by the fact that when she looked at herself and then looked at her, she felt embarrassed by the difference and therefore decided finally not to come out but to monitor what happened outside from one corner of her bedroom. The crowd increased as the news of their arrival spread across the town. Fanta came forward and attempted to shake Sakayo's hand but he quickly put his hand to his chest and Fanta came to herself and did the same and smiled, realizing her mistake and asked him to move the car to the chief's second house. He obeyed and moved it across many houses whilst she directed him from inside the car. They arrived at the house and occupied it. Fanta shuttled between her house and the lodge bringing food and water and other necessary items. She got everything arranged and it was then time for the visitors to eat. Sakayo was worried that he had not seen Nema and his mind was completely occupied with her absence. May be he was wrong not to have entered his own house to see who was there at that time. But he was told that there were only three of them in the house and he had seen two of them when they came out and greeted him. What could have happened that he could not see her? Was she sick and could not come out?

Entona could have told him that almost immediately when they met. He could not find answers to most of the questions which occupied his mind at the moment. He could neither rest properly nor was he comfortable with Nema's absence from the scene. Finally, he asked Kaye to accompany him to his father'shouse. They drove and arrived there, parked the car, and went into the house. He looked for Nema and she was there on the chair where she used to sit and gave instructions to him about what to do. He went and embraced her without taking any precautions "Good to see you Aunty", he said. "Welcome home," replied Nema. "How is Mary doing?" He asked politely. "She is doing quite well. I am pleased with her performance." she said. "Aunty, we are happy to find all of you in good health. We are going to see some other people around the neighborhood, we will see you later" Sakayo said and they left for the lodge. At the Lodge they ate and had more visitors. The last visitors were the chief and a young man. "Sakayo, this is the young man whose life you saved from the mango tree" said the chief. "Suku, how are you? I always recall the dramatic way the solution came to save your life. You have grown up. At Which level are you in school?" he enquired. "I have completed the West African Senior Secondary School Certificate Examinations (WASSSCE), and I am looking forward to enrolling in college shortly," he said. "Good, you have done well. Chief, thank you very much for your support to him;" he said happily. "Sakayo, we are proud of you. Right from your childhood you proved beyond doubt that you would be a good person and we have seen it. Tomorrow we have a reception for you, your mother and your friend in your former school. Please come over there and enjoy yourselves and don't hesitate to tell us what we are doing wrong out here in Kayima" the chief requested. "Thank you chief" and turning to the young man he said, "Let us talk before I leave the town. Thank you so much and good night", he said and saw them to the door.

The next day whilst Betty entertained the visitors at the lodge Sakayo and Kaye went around the town looking for friends and acquaintances and indeed they found some of them and they spent quite some time talking to them at various locations in the town.

They also visited some particular sites around the town where they normally went to fetch firewood. They noticed that the trees had been cut down substantially and the beauty that the forest provided when they were in school was no longer there. They returned to the lodge and got ready for the reception. Sakayo brought out all the personal gifts and the books, pens and pencils for the school. He marked every envelope that contained a gift and put them in order in his handbag. He allowed Betty to present the dresses in accordance with the names he had discussed with her. The gifts to his father and Nema were special and kept aside for him to present. He and Kaye drove to his house again, where he presented Entona an envelope containing some money, a carton of assorted items, dresses for Nema plus a wrist watch. In the carton were dresses for Mary, shoes, books, pens and pencils. Entona received the items and entrusted everything to Nema before the two young men left to get ready for the reception. Entona and Nema then got ready and walked out of their house in good time. But at some reasonable distance away from the house she told him that she was not comfortable in the mauve dress. She felt it was not good enough for that occasion. They returned home and searched her suitcase and brought out another dress which she put on and looked at herself in a mirror. She was not satisfied with it either. And she went again into the suitcase and brought out yet another dress. She took her time to dress up whilst he waited patiently. When she dressed up finally he could not see the difference for which she spent so much time. They arrived very late for the reception and occupied their seats. When everything was in place, the chief got up and informed the house that the occasion was not for speech making but for eating and drinking, in honor of the visitors, Sakayo who was now an Engineer and Kaye, an Immigration officer, and of course Betty a potential nurse in the Making. She would be a blessing to any community wherever she found herself, he informed his audience.

He announced that service of the food must commence the moment he stopped speaking, and indeed service commenced almost immediately he stopped speaking. The school hall was completely full and the service was well organized with a lot of goat meat, chickens and fish cooked with cassava leaves or pepper soup. Although the hall was full yet everyone was served the various kinds of food that was available. Betty sat close to the table occupied by Sakayo and Kaye. She enjoyed every service and felt very good about the honor given to her son. She was directly opposite Entona and Nema. She could see that Entona was joyful despite his ill health. She did not know Nema well enough so she could not tell from her facial expression whether she was really happy. What she realized was that she stared at her very often to the notice of some people sitting close to her. Whenever she spoke she listened very keenly and concentrated on what she said. She could not tell why she concentrated so much on her. Before the end of the reception Sakayo got up and thanked the chief and all the organizers. He promised that he would always be by their side in their development efforts. He then presented the school with many cartons of books, pens and pencils. He gave special gifts to the chief, to Yaja his former teacher and to many friends and acquaintances. Betty too presented many dresses to the women in the name of her son. The reception was unique and ended very well. The news of his visit and the reception went far and wide in Sandoh. Every parent or guardian was happy that even a poor man's child could be educated to the level of Sakayo. The occasion renewed the strength of all farmers in the area to cultivate more land and earn enough money to support their children's education.

The next morning was the departure time. The crowd around the lodge that morning was bigger than the crowd at their arrival. The difference between the two gatherings was that most people in the crowd that morning had brought along either a piece of cocoa yam, a live chicken, some rice neatly tied in a piece of cloth, some bananas or some dried meat to give to Sakayo.

It was indeed a successful trip and all of them enjoyed it. Before he left Kayima he called Entona aside and gave him enough money and encouraged him to come over to Freetown for an urgent medical check-up. He also gave him his telephone number in case there was a need to talk to him whenever the need arose. The car left Kayima late that day because he spoke to virtually everybody that was present that morning. At the end of it all he was so exhausted that Kaye drove the car all the way to Freetown. Most of the time he and Betty slept but Kaye was such a good driver that there was no hiccup anywhere throughout the journey. They arrived late at night and stayed together until the next day when Kaye went home and prepared for work.

In Kayima Entona and Nema sat down together to distribute the dresses and books among friends and relatives after Mary had got a reasonable share. They started it well until she intimated that the best thing that Sakayo should do was to take Mary along to Freetown. "This is a good idea. But who do you think is his cook?" he asked. "Leave that to him to determine. He is matured enough to determine who should cook for his sister," Nema responded angrily. "No, we must look at the issue realistically. Betty is his cook now. Do you expect her to prepare food for your child, and you think there is nothing wrong with that?" He asked with anxiety in his

125

voice. "Will Betty stay with him forever?" she asked in turn. "That is a question for him, not for me. But what is wrong if she stays with her son permanently?" he argued. "So, are you implying he must not get a wife and settle down?" She said. These are his exact words when I contacted him on marriage, Entona explained to her.

"Marriage requires time and must be entered into with the right kind of person after a lot of spiritual and physical preparations. When I am up to that standard I will" reported Entona.

"So as a matter of fact no one can push Betty out or push Sakayo into an early marriage. For now, it makes a lot of sense for Mary to stay with us and accept any support from him in respect of her," he stated firmly. "But in all of these, have you made any suggestions to him and listen to what he will say concerning her? You have failed to do so," she pointed out.

"Yes, you are right. I have not made any suggestions so far because I don't want to make any unreasonable requests. The issues are clear and simple," he replied. "This is an endorsement that Mary should not get the education she needs. It shows how fair you are," she remarked. "I love Mary and her progress," he said and moved out of the house in an unhappy mood. A week later Entona's health deteriorated. He coughed and had sleepless nights. The circumstances forced him to make an early journey to Freetown. He had his clothes laundered which he neatly packed in his suitcase and left enough money with Nema and his son's telephone number, in case of any unforeseen circumstances. She was very suspicious about his journey. She did not think the illness was the only reason that was pushing him to go. When she examined his suitcase before he left, she

126

found he had taken all his best clothes along as if he was not coming back. And above all, he talked much about the trip to his friends as if it was a pleasure trip. She knew he was hiding something from her but she remembered quite well her grandmother's famous parable that "You cannot hide an object under your armpit in a boxing competition. Surely it will come out and fall down as the competition proceeds," she consoled herself. So in like manner Entona's secrets would be revealed to everyone much to his surprise.

Entona boarded the earliest bus to Freetown from Koidu town, where he had spent the night. That morning his concentration was divided. His illness worried him and he knew he had lost a lot of weight and his appetite was not improving. But he was confident that once he was in Freetown his son would ensure he got the best medical attention. Secondly, he was not sure what Betty's reaction would be to him after many years of separation. Would she treat him callously or would she have sympathy for him as a sick man? What would Sakayo do? Would he try to reconcile them? He was convinced that a discussion of that nature may have taken place between the two already but he would not know which way it went. But if reconciliation became possible because of his intervention, that would be the beginning of his problems. It would mean contending with two wives which would run contrary to his faith. If the principle of the sequence of arrival was used as a basis of judgment, Betty would stay and Nema would go. But where would she go and what would happen to Mary? These thoughts occupied his mind so much that he was surprised when the apprentice to the driver announced, "Any passengers for waterloo?" Half an hour later he was

127

in Freetown. He checked Sakayo's address and hired a taxi which took him to Bass Street. Betty was alone at home when he arrived. She got him some hot water to wash and whilst he was in the bathroom she arranged one of the rooms for him. She served food when he was ready for it. Later she served him tea and lime and sat with him in the parlor until Sakayo returned from work. The next morning Sakayo took Entona to hospital where he went through a series of laboratory tests. He was asked to repeat some of the tests after a month according to the examination and he was advised in his own best interest to avoid all types of alcohol. Entona was quick to ask the doctor whether palm wine could be a threat to his life. "You are absolutely correct. Do you know that water and sugar are added to the pure palm wine to increase the volume in order to make more money?" asked the doctor. "Yes", he said. "Now, you will agree with me that natural palm wine is very rare these days. What we have is palm wine diluted with water and some quantity of sugar to maintain its taste. The water used is mostly from streams, swamps or rivers. You will agree with me too that such water is hardly pure. Besides this point, each time you drink such palm wine you are forced to take in more sugar which you do not need. Obviously, the impure water and the excess sugar will create diseases that will threaten your life," explained the doctor.

Entona listened attentively as the doctor analyzed the consequences of drinking diluted palm wine. He agreed with him on virtually all the points that he raised. He thought about the analysis in his quiet moment and decided he would quit drinking palm wine when he recovered. But then he realized that the Entire Bassama Club was his making. What would the other members feel

128

when he finally quits? Whilst he recuperated his mind remained fully occupied with when and how to leave Bassama as his mind was made up to quit drinking. Sakayo bought all the drugs according to the prescription and handed them to Betty, who was better placed to administer them to him, based on her ongoing professional training as a nurse at the Connaught Hospital. Entona went to bed immediately after receiving some doses of the medicines. For the first three days he slept for most of the time. He woke up to eat or to go to the rest room and back to bed. After a week the coughing stopped but his appetite was still not good. But as he continued his treatment into the second week he started eating well and feeling strong. One day Entona came out of his room and sat face to face with Betty.

"Thank you for your support," he said. "Okay, but it is your son who is doing everything for you. I am just playing the role of a woman in the home, in the absence of his wife," she explained.

"I am sorry for what happened between us. I need forgiveness," he continued. "I have forgiven not just you but Nema as well for whatever happened to me. I count everything as gain to me. I have also told Sakayo to consider Mary as his blood relative who had no part to play in whatever happened between us, the parents. I have emphasized that he should help her out whenever the opportunity arose," She explained.

Entona went into his room and wept behind closed doors. He tried but could not find any reason why he had asked Betty out of his house then. While he was still in the room there was a knock on his door. "Entona, it is time for your next dose of medicine," she informed him.

When he came out later Betty noticed that his eyes were unusually red. "Your eyes are red. Did you attempt to sleep just now?" she enquired. "No, I did not sleep. I was reflecting on the past," he said. "No, you must try to live in the present, especially for your health," she advised when she concluded that he wept in his room.

Back home in Kayima Nema was confused. There were no pieces of information with respect to Entona's illness and treatment. But much more of concern to her was that both Betty and Entona were staying together in Sakayo's house. She knew he loved his parents and would try to reconcile them. She got herself prepared for a day's journey to see Sokiti. She was quite familiar with the footpath because she had been there many times to see him. She had contacted him at the early part of her relationship with Entona and she believed that it was his intervention that helped to get the relationship right. But the relationship had become shaky with the return of Sakayo. She convinced herself that she needed to see him again and she got herself prepared for the journey. Nothing could hold her back because she needed to get the relationship right once and for all. After a long walk she arrived in Bandaya at the time when most people returned from their farms. Sokiti found her on his veranda in the company of his two wives. She waited until he went into his room, got prepared and then asked her to come in. "What is the problem again?" asked Sokiti as soon as she entered.

"Sakayo, Entona's son has returned from America. Betty is staying with him in Freetown and Entona has gone there for medical treatment. I have no doubt that Sakayo wants to reconcile them," she said. "When is he coming back home?" asked Sokiti. "I don't know when," she said. "You have to ensure that he comes back soon, otherwise how are you going to dose his food or drink, to get his mind back to you? We will not achieve anything as long as he stays away from you. Anyway, put these pieces of herbs in his food or drink whenever you have access to him. You know exactly what to do because you have done it before," he said. Nema took out some money from her purse and put it on the mat on which he sat and Sokiti checked it and put it back. "Why have you maintained my pay the same as when you first saw me? Have you been to the market recently? Prices have gone up, please make some addition," he requested. Nema opened her purse again and brought out some money and laid it on the mat. "Thank you very much. You know, I take a lot of risks to satisfy you. Our work entails dealing with demons and my life is always in danger. This is why we ask for a lot of money as compensation," he explained. Nema returned to Kayima the next morning and she located the telephone number which Entona left with her. She sent a message to her friend in the neighborhood and asked her to look after Mary whilst she was away at Koidu town. She did not use any mobile telephone in Kayima because she wanted to keep their conversation secret and hide her emotions from her friends and relatives and to tell Entona that Mary's food had finished. She left with the first vehicle and within two hours she was in Koidu town. She walked down the road to access the Tele centre which was located near the Post Office.At the Tele centre she requested to make a call to Freetown, and she paid the charges and waited for her turn. The numbers were dialed and she was on line. Sakayo's telephone rang and Betty ran across the room

131

quickly and answered. "Hello, Sakayo's house," she asked. "You want to talk to Entona? Who are you? Oh! it is you Nema. I am sorry; you cannot talk to him now. He has taken his medicines and he is asleep, and the doctor warned us not to wake him up for any reason. I am sorry to hear that Mary hasn't enough food left at home. This is serious enough, we will ask Sakayo to send some money for food tomorrow. Oh, you want to know when he will be coming back. Well, the doctor has asked for a repeat of some of the tests for now. Beyond that, you have to talk to him. You want to talk to him in the evening. No, you cannot talk to him any time today. The best time will be tomorrow before 10 am." She explained. There was a click on the line and Betty could no longer hear her voice. Nema was furious that Betty could not allow her to talk to Entona. Was he so sick that he could not stand up for a few minutes? She also said he would not return home now because he had to repeat some tests. She felt that those statements were made up to keep him permanently in Freetown. She was not satisfied with the pieces of information that she got from Betty and so she decided to pass the night in Koidu town in-order to hear from him in the morning. She located a lodge with a former school mate around the post office and the next day she was at the telecenter very early indeed. She paid the charges and she was on line. "Hello, this is Entona. How are you Nema?" he asked. "You want me to come home now? You have not asked how I am doing; you just want me to come over immediately because there is not enough food at home. What happened to the money I left for food? Yes the cost of living is high, but I made enough provision. Anyway, we have asked Sakayo to send some money to you right now as I speak to you. You

132

know what is keeping me in Freetown! What is it? Reconciled with Betty! Sakayo has reconciled us! Please talk something sensible. You want me to come now! I am going to obey the doctor and stay as long as he wants me to stay in order to get my health back. If I don't come now that will be the end of our relationship!! It is impossible for me to come now. My health is crucially important to me," he said and hung up. Betty listened keenly to the conversation and when he hung up she came close to him and whispered, "Is it true that Sakayo has reconciled us? "Reconciled us?" he exclaimed. "It is Nema who said it," he explained.

Chapter Nine

The Secret Revealed

Nema waited patiently on the counter of the First International Bank in Koidu town until she received the sum of Five hundred thousand Leones ($67), sent by Sakayo in fulfillment of his promise to her and Mary. She put the money in the inner pocket of her hand bag and walked out of the Bank to the street. She was in a hurry and appeared to be unhappy about the conversation she had with Entona. It was like talking to some strange person. The conversation did not reflect any intimacy and cordiality and sounded too formal and brief. Her face revealed anger and her entire body became weak and it appeared like she was losing out to Betty. She wondered what could have happened to cause Entona to treat her like a stranger. Could it have been the influence of Betty or Sakayo? She wondered and kept on analyzing every sentence of the conversation as she walked to the Kayima Lorry Park. Confused, she stopped suddenly and looked around as if she was expecting to see somebody out there. Her eyes were wide open and her expression thoughtful. She weighed the possibility of travelling to Freetown to be part of whatever was happening out there between them. But the thought of Mary without a complete motherly care caused her to change her mind quickly. She continued her journey to the Lorry Park in a rather sad mood because she felt strongly that Entona and Betty were about to reunite. Anger moved through her body causing her eyes to water up and tears to flow down her cheeks. Suddenly she came to herself and realized she was in a public place. She took out her handkerchief and wiped her tears away, leaving her eyes red and noticeable. In the Lorry Park, she engaged the driver of the land rover and got a seat directly behind him. She wanted a seat that had enough space around it for her long legs. She sat in the seat and moved her legs freely in the space around it. She was happy because she had avoided cramps of her legs which could have caused her some pains over a long distance. When she settled down in her seat, she looked around to see who was in there with her and she found four other ladies and a young man who sat close to her. The ladies were busy arranging their luggage under their seats whilst the young man was busy urging the driver to step up his search for additional passengers so that the journey could start as early as possible. He looked at his wrist watch perpetually as if there was an agreed departure time. There was nothing like that. Departure depended on having the full capacity of ten passengers in the vehicle. Already there were two in the front seat and six in the cabin. The driver needed two additional passengers. He and his teenage apprentice made frantic efforts to convince a group of undecided passengers to join their vehicle. Two of the passengers made up their minds and joined them whilst the others waited for the other vehicles that plied the same route. The additional two male passengers topped the number to ten. When the passengers boarded the vehicle, the apprentice brought out a small square bench and forced it in the small space available between the feet of the passengers.

Then the driver placed the key in the starter and there was a big sound that followed. As it moved away it left a trail of the black smoke which thinned out as it moved further away along the route to Kayima. The passengers were quite satisfied about the early departure which would give them the opportunity to reach their destination in good time. Nema adjusted herself on her seat and focused on the issues that affected her life. Her angry accusations of Entona and the entire conversation repeated themselves in her mind as the vehicle trudged along the gravel road past Yengema Town. Her chain of thought was broken when the vehicle ran into a deep pot hole that rocked it left to right, almost throwing every passenger onto the floor of the cabin. "Stop, stop," cried the young man. "Do you want o kill us?" screamed the other passengers together. The driver slowed down, apologized and continued driving at that pace until he crossed the multiple pot holes onto a smooth sandy road that stretched a few kilometers ahead of them. When normalcy returned in the vehicle, the conversations with Betty repeated themselves in Nema's mind again. She tried to give a meaning to every word or expression in the conversation. Finally she concluded that Entona and Betty would be reunited simply because Sakayo would not support him if he did not reconcile with his mother. That conclusion brought a sharp paralyzing pain to her head. She breathed heavily to release the pressure in her head and looked outside the vehicle to concentrate on the beauty of the vegetation on the mountains and valleys along the route. She realized they were already in Sedu, very close o Yormadu Town. She looked forward to a stop-over in Yormadu so that she could disembark and attend to nature. The vehicle climbed a little hill from the Baffin Bridge and went right up to the market, which happened to be in the centre of the town. The passengers climbed out of the vehicle and moved in different directions to different homes that would accommodate them to attend to nature. Yormadu meant the town ahead of other towns or the next town after a particular town. It was a big town both in terms of area and population and it was located on a hill side over-looking the black river called Baffin, which contained precious gold and diamonds, and crocodiles. To take the gold and diamonds one had to keep shut the devastating jaws of the beasts or cope with the force of the river. Many took the precious stones away safely, escaping the force of the river and the man-eaters but others remained in the river forever, either due to its force or taken away by crocodiles. Despite these threats more and more people came to the town in search of quick wealth. The river bed had been scraped over and the top soil around the town had been turned over and over. Yet new comers were satisfied and confident to repeat what was done year in and year out because they had hope of getting better precious stones than their predecessors. The driver sounded the horn and all the passengers rushed towards the vehicle and took their seats. The young man was still making calls on his cell phone. He completed his calls and joined the vehicle before it sped off. Nema looked refreshed and calm after the break but Betty occupied her mind constantly. She tried to throw her out of her mind during the short break but she remained there. Then she made up her mind that she would do anything it would take to get her out of Entona's life. The moment the driver left Yormadu his attention was forcibly drawn to Tegbadu hill, which was well known by most drivers. It was a long, awkward, and steep which had caused many accidents. The passengers knew the hill just like the drivers did. The passengers would normally disembark and allow the driver and his apprentice to be on board the vehicle whilst descending the hill. But the driver decided to keep the passengers on board during the descent. The passengers held tightly to whatever their hands came in contact with. The squall and crunch of the metal brakes could be heard afar off. The vehicle went left, right and then centre as if it was controlling itself. But of course, the driver was in control, although the smooth front tyres made the control process difficult. Then the vehicle went straight down as if the brakes had failed but in the middle of the hill the speed reduced, implying that they were working. The driver struggled with the steering and perspired from head to toe, making his clothes look like newly laundered clothes. He yelled out for his apprentice to run down the hill and tell him whether to drive left or right of the big rock ahead of him. The apprentice ran quickly ahead and pointed to the left. And with an incredible speed the vehicle rode to the left and got into several pot holes which bounced it up and down many times. The shrill and high pitched voices of the passengers echoed through the forest before the vehicle stopped at the bottom of the hill safely. When it was all quiet in the vehicle, the passengers got up and agitated to climb down in anger, but the driver apologized again and assured them that nothing like that would happen again. He encouraged them to sit down so that he could get them to their destination quickly. When the vehicle took off, the incident became fun and laughter for each and everyone on board.

Nema, who kept to herself most of the time, spoke passionately about how she felt during the descent. Everyone spoke about their experience. It was indeed a lively debate which lasted long. By the time they had said all that they wanted to say, they were already in Kayima Town. All the passengers paid their transport fares and moved to their various homes. Nema found Mary playing handball with other children outside their house. They came out of the game and embraced her warmly. They took her handbag from her and walked behind her, very hopeful to have some gifts. Nema noticed their desire and opened her handbag and brought out some biscuits which she shared among them. She spoke to Mary about her meals which she confirmed she had on a regular basis and praised aunt Hawa for being kind to her. Hawa Sebengu was a tall beautiful young lady who was much younger than Nema with a stable married life despite the challenges she and her family faced as subsistent rice farmers. She gave all the support her husband needed as a farmer and she co-operated fully with family members and friends in the neighborhood. One such person she worked with earnestly was Nema. They exchanged many things common to both families. For instance, they exchanged husk rice for a minimum sum of money. When Hawa wanted husk rice but did not have enough money to pay for it; Nema gave them enough to plough. When Nema was on a trip outside Kayima, Hawa would take care of Mary. The relationship worked well between them. Hawa worked hard on the farm which made her beauty not to be noticeable at first sight. The hard work made her slimmer with rough palms and bony cheeks. But when examined closely, her beauty revealed naturally: the fine set of white teeth, the lovely thick black hair and the bulging beautiful bulging eyes. She got married at the early age of fifteen and nearly after ten years, she had five children; three boys and two girls, all attending school. That was what kept her close to the farm, to grow crops and market them for school fees. She heard about Nema's return and she went over to greet her. When she arrived there, she went straight into her bedroom where she was resting. "It is good that you have come. I was just planning to send Mary to call you. Did she give you a hell of a time?" she asked. "You know that she is always well behaved. No, I did not have any problems with her," she said. Nema got up and asked Mary to go out and play with her friends. Then she closed the door, leaving only the two of them inside. "My sister, my marriage is in trouble. I need your advice right now. Sakayo's return from the United States of America is about to reunite Entona and his former wife Betty", she claimed with tears running down her cheeks. "Sakayo has pronounced him to be very sick and has taken him to Freetown for medical attention. Now the three of them are living under the same roof, giving them the opportunity to forgive each other and reunite", she continued. "I need your advice, something that will help me to retain him. I can't do without him, especially for Mary's schooling", she said and wept. Hawa's eyes fluttered in amazement. She got up from the chair and sat close to her on the bed. She held her on the shoulder and spoke softly into her left ear. "Be careful about what you do and say in such a situation. First of all, try to get in touch with Entona on his cell phone now. Sympathize with him and ask whether he is getting better and inform him that Mary is missing him a lot. Ask him to suggest what to do with respect to that. Don't accuse him for things that are still rumors and tell him that you are on top of the situation back home. Suggest to him that you would like to come and see him, and send greetings to both Sakayo and Betty, and wish him a speedy recovery. Once you do this you will be better guided in whatever moves you may wish to take," she said and waited for her reaction. "Thank you very much. I know that you are speaking to me from the bottom of your heart and from experience. I would have taken the steps that you have suggested if it were a normal situation. I am quite convinced that Betty is using some extra ordinary powers to attract Entona to herself, quite apart from her son's return. Therefore, there is a need for me to counter whatever she is doing to take him away from her. I am sorry if I do not use your steps because I need him at all cost," she said almost shouting. Hawa empathized with her when she tried to put herself in her shoes, but on a second thought she knew Betty very well and doubted very much whether she would indulge in such things which Nema was accusing her of. She knew her to be a simple person who was always happy in her marriage whether it was for good or bad. She got up and wished her the best in her attempt to get her husband back. She bid her farewell and walked home still meditating on what she wanted to do. She was not familiar with the occult world. She believed in hard work and good working relationship with everybody. She had respect for her husband and did not police him wherever he went. Nema spent most of the day in her bedroom with her mind fully occupied with Entona and Betty. She lay on her bed until Mary knocked on her door and informed her that Hawa had sent a big basin of food for her. It was at that moment she got up and gave Mary her share and left some quantity in the basin for herself as she was not hungry. She was still busy planning what to do to prevent Betty and Entona from reconciling. Night fell suddenly like a curtain being dropped. She remained on her bed until the early morning sunlight poured in through the window and penetrated on her eyes and she woke up with a start. It was at that moment that she realized she was late to prepare breakfast. She got up and prepared breakfast in a hurry consisting of some loaves of bread and two tins of sardine which she had bought in Koidu town. She had breakfast with Mary, went into her room and got ready for a journey. She asked her to stay at home whilst she was away and promised that she would not stay long. She took her handbag and went across the town towards the northern section. She arrived at a house at the extreme end of the town, very close to the grave yard and knocked on the front door. The door creaked open and a tall shabby man showed up. He was thin with a long beard that was turning grey. His smile revealed his brown teeth with two missing in the upper jaw, leaving a big gap there. His eye lashes were grey and his head was either bald or clean shaven. His arms were long to match his height, with very long fingers on a big palm. He could be mistaken for a basket ball star but he was not. He was a soothsayer and an occultist with many years of practice in towns on the border between Guinea and Sierra Leone. He was Nonko Serifu and he was new in Kayima. News about him spread quickly by his new clients, who had helped to propagate the good news about his extraordinary solutions for the sick, the bewitched, restoration of broken marriages and the like.

He invited Nema into his bedroom and made her sit on the only available chair in the room whilst he sat on a mat in the center of the room. She looked around quickly and made her case: "Somebody told me that you could be a solution to broken marriages. Mine is on the verge of being broken. This is why I am here," she said and waited for his reaction. And suddenly there was a knock on the door and the permission was granted by Nonko, the host. Then a young man entered and greeted them. The voice was familiar and Nema turned around to view the person that had entered and discovered that he was the young man she travelled with a day ago. "Posua, please wait outside. I will talk to you later" said Nonko and Posua stepped backwards and disappeared from the room. "Yes madam, your name and your story, and make sure you state clearly what you intend to achieve" he instructed and waited. "I have a daughter with Entona and we have stayed together for many years. But before I met him, he had a son with Betty. I took care of the child until he had the opportunity to travel abroad. The boy has returned home and has taken Entona, his father to Freetown for medical attention. But Betty is staying with him in Freetown. Now Entona and Betty are staying under the same roof with Sakayo as their host. I sense that Sakayo is trying to reunite them and leave me out with my daughter. I want you to help me stop the reunion and bring him back home immediately," she explained. "What you have asked me to do is not difficult. A lot depends on your co-operation from the beginning to the end of a process that I shall introduce. It will also depend on your moral strength. To begin with, I need a young boy to receive your messages right now and secondly I need a fee of five hundred thousand Leones ($67)", he said emphatically. Nema went out solemnly and tried to figure out where to get the young boy. Her mind ran straight to Saafea, a young boy whose parents were dead and who stayed with a relative that did not care much about his welfare. She walked to the Lorry Park where he hung out most of the time. She searched everywhere in the Park but he could not be found there. She went to the football pitch and found him on the bench whilst his team played on. She stood behind him and asked him to follow her.

He followed her hoping to return to the pitch soon. Somewhere along the road she stood and handed over to him the sum of Five Thousand Leones ($0.67). "Thank you very much madam. Where do you intend to send me?" he asked but she did not reply. She walked faster and beckoned on him to follow. He was happy for being in possession of five thousand Leones and followed her without any hesitation. He was quite sure that his lunch was settled for many days to come. He kept the Five Thousand Leones in his right trousers pocket and tied the inside bottom of the pocket with a piece of rope for additional protection. They were already in front of a house, and Nema was still leading the way. They entered the verandah and she knocked on the door.

Posua came out and left the door open. He worked as an Acting Accountant in the Koidu Mining Company Limited. The position of accountant was advertised and he had filed his application but he was still looking for other means to ensure that he got the position. He worked hard and his employer knew it very well, but he lacked confidence in the system. When he came out of the room he recognized Nema as Sakayo's aunt. He remembered Sakayo very well and the weekly class competitions they had in their primary school which they enjoyed very much. He knew that he was out of the country for quite some time and had returned recently as a full fledge engineer. He recalled too that he met him during his first visit to his parents in Kayima where they had exchanged cell phone numbers but they had never called each other since then. He came to Kayima to see Nonko the soothsayer who had influenced the career development of some of his friends. He wanted to grow in his career as well and that was why he was in Nonko's house that morning. But he was surprised to have found Nema out there. What was she trying to achieve with Nonko? He could not find appropriate answers, and so ignored her presence and tried to concentrate on his own affairs. He had applied for the post of accountant in the Koidu Mining Company. The advert was open to the public which made him quite uncomfortable. That was why he came to see Nonko to do everything possible in his power to get him the job. Whilst he sat down trying to figure out what may have happened, Nema and Saafea entered into Nonko's bedroom, next to the room where he was lodged for the night. Nema sat on the only available chair in the bedroom and Saafea was asked to sit on the matt, which was right in the centre of the bedroom. "What is your name", asked Nonko.

"My name is Saafea Danaya", he replied in a sharp youthful voice.

"Listen to me keenly; you are here to receive messages and to pass them on to me. Don't be afraid of anything, nobody is going to harm you. Take this card and hold it before your face continuously", he ordered. Saafea took the plain square cardboard from him and did as he instructed. Nonko then began to turn the ring of beads held together by a strong ream of thread which passed through the hole in each bead. He turned the beads in his right palm, skillfully, touching each of them and enchanting some strange words as each bead was touched. Saafea concentrated on the card and so did Nema. Looking on the card, his eyes grew dimmer and dimmer until he shouted aloud and cried for help. He dropped the card and attempted to escape but Nonko's strong hands held him firmly in the same position. "Whatever you see, please ask him to sit down on the chair available to him. Don't be afraid, he said. Saafea was forced to sit down to do what he was told. "It is too fearful. I cannot bear his sight. Please let me go, let me go", he wept. "Tell him to sit down and listen to him", ordered Nonko. "Please sit down", he spoke to what he saw on the card but still complained that he did not understand what he was saying to him. "Talk to him the language you understand", said Nonko. Saafea told him that he understood only Kono language and thereafter a lengthy communication commenced between them immediately. He kept his face straight before the card. He could not do otherwise but to look and listen. He got the message from the image, and passed them on to Nonko as he received them. "He says to break the reunion between Entona and Betty; she needs old clothes of Entona (shirt or trousers), a red cock, fifty red kola nuts, a ring and some dried pepper. He says further that she must dig a hole in their sitting room to a reasonable depth and bury the cock alive, with all the other items. He says that nobody should know what she has done and nobody should open the hole which must be completely sealed. He says that the consequences of disclosure of any part of or the entire secret would cost somebody his life," Saafea narrated. Nonko took the card away from him when the messages stopped flowing and thanked him for a job well done. Nema thanked him too and bid him farewell. Saafea walked out of the room quickly and ran towards the football pitch, hoping to find some of his friends there. As he ran he touched the bottom of his pocket and felt the Five Thousand Leones. He was happy that his lunch for the next one week in school was completely addressed. He wondered when next such good luck would come his way. He recalled that on his seventh birthday his father bought him some clothes and gave him a cash gift of eight thousand Leones. It was immediately after that occasion that the war came to their town and many houses were burnt down, including theirs. It was in that confusion that he was separated from his parents. There were many rumors about their whereabouts but nobody was successful to see them face to face. Some said that his mother was killed and his father was alive but could not come home because they lost everything back home and had the feeling that all their siblings were dead. Each year brought its own stories or lies but the truth was that they never came back. He had been living with his father's cousin since that fateful day of the war. He arrived at the football pitch and joined the winning team. He never tried to be alone after his experience with the lady that gave her the five thousand Leones. Whenever he was alone, he recalled the image, and he would run to any group of people around him. The image troubled his life for a long time but he refused to tell anybody because the image said that anyone who disclosed the secret would not live but die suddenly. Nema was still in the room listening to Nonko. "Have you understood every bit of the instructions? You must not make any mistakes and you must ensure it remains top secret. Madness, blindness and death are the punishment for disclosure of the secret. As a result you are expected to be alone in the house on the day you wish to carry out the instructions and it must take place by midnight when your neighbors are asleep", Nonko instructed. "Now give me five hundred thousand Leones $67). I know that you are a poor woman that is why I have charged that minimum sum," he said. Nema scratched her head and opened her handbag and counted the sum of three hundred thousand Leones ($40) only and handed it over to him. "Good. You are expected to come back to me when you are successful and to pay the remaining sum. And if there are any problems anywhere let me know", he assured her. "When I do everything accordingly, how will I know it has worked? What would be the sign?" She asked. Nonko smiled and shook his head. "When I put enmity between Entona and Betty, it would not be a secret. There will be a big dispute beyond human understanding. They will never come together as husband and wife", he assured her. Nema went home satisfied that she was on the right path to success. The next day she went to the market and bought some food for the day's cooking and then bought all the items required for the sacrifice. She returned home within a short time and went into the kitchen. Shortly afterwards a cloud of white smoke rose above the kitchen and sweet smells of good food accompanied the smoke into the air. The sweet smell drew Mary and her friends to the house and into the kitchen. Children enjoy food when they eat together like in a competition. They received their shares and took their positions and emptied their plates. They were full and hoped the sauce would be repeated before the end of the week. Back in the sitting room in the evening, Mary and her friends sang popular school songs and narrated stories until it was time for them to go back to their respective homes. Nema cleaned upthe dishes and packed the kitchen neatly before going to her bedroom. She checked on the cock and the other items which were kept in the room reserved for visitors. She was quite satisfied with the arrangements so far and looked forward to midnight to implement what she was asked to do. Nema was convinced that it was the right thing to do to regain Entona. She recalled that she found it very difficult to locate a husband initially. How could she allow herself to lose him in a careless manner? As part of the arrangements, she told Mary that she was going on a short trip to a nearby village where she intended to pass the night. She informed her that she would pass the night at Aunt Hawa's house. Before the end of the day she spoke to Hawa on the issue and got her approval and before it got dark, she escorted Mary to Aunt Hawa's house where they were lodged in one of the vacant rooms the same she had slept in when her mother went on a short trip recently. She returned home quickly and closed the doors and windows to every room and got into her bedroom. From the outside it appeared as if there was nobody inside. That was what she wanted the neighbors to assume and indeed she got them to think that way. She remained inside the house being very careful not to drop anything for anybody to suspect that somebody was there. She waited patiently for midnight to approach. She peeped through the cracks in the windows to determine the movement of people in the neighborhood, especially around the house close to hers. The movements got less as darkness covered the neighborhood completely. The only light she could see from inside was the light from fire flies moving about in the open space or roof tops. The entire environment was quiet except for the voices of owls in the trees at the back of the houses. When she was convinced that it was midnight she opened the main door and peeped to see who was there. But there was nobody except her neighbor's dog which barked once or twice and ran across to her, waged its tail and ran back to its hide out on the neighbor's verandah. She closed the door quietly and went into her bedroom and got ready for the

149

operation. She went into the store and brought out a pick axe and a big hoe and went to the sitting room. She removed the chairs and the carpet and identified the site for the hole. She dug skillfully, avoiding loud sounds. It was a difficult task altogether to dig the hole without making a noise. She took a long time but eventual dug the hole after many hours. She brought the items into the sitting from where she kept them. And without wasting any time, she placed the pepper, the kola nuts, clothes and then the cock. She struggled a little bit to force the cock into the hole with its wings held firmly and disallowed from making any movements. Notwithstanding the force that was applied on it some noise could be heard at a close range, although it died out as the hole was filled completely with mud and sand. She sweated profusely after the exercise and she opened one of the windows to allow a flow of cool air into the sitting room. Nema placed the chair close to the window and immediately her body started to cool down as the sweat dried up quickly. Whilst she was enjoying the cool breeze, she started to nod. She got up and closed the window and went to bed. She had an undisturbed sleep until the early hours of the morning when she woke up with a start. She had a dream in which she saw the cock flying out of the window. She got up and went quietly and quickly into the sitting room to see how the cock managed to get out. But she found the seal intact as she left it and she felt satisfied. Two days after the digging ceremony she made an attempt to test the power of the sacrifice she had made. She made a call to Entona through a friend's cell phone. The call lasted only a few minutes but brought joy and happiness to the family because Entona received the call and spoke to her as if everything was normal. He informed her that he was responding to treatment and eating very well. He advised her to take good care of Mary whilst he was away, and promised to return home as soon as his doctor was satisfied with his medical condition. He bid her farewell and then hung up. She came home running and full of joy. She gave the news to Mary and she was happy that her father was coming back home soon. She missed him a lot. There was joy in the family because of the good news. The neighbors knew something good had happened in Entona's house because Mary told everybody around them that her father was coming soon. Many people in the town felt that Entona was so sick that he could not make it but the confidence displayed by Mary made them believe too that he was well and about to return home.

Posua was in Kayima to see Nonko, ahead of his interview for the post of Accountant at Koidu Mining Company Limited, where he had worked for the last three years. He was a diligent worker and had no problems with his duties and responsibilities. He dealt with colleagues with care and understood their importance as team mates because he had read the book "The One Minute Manager" many times and it helped him a lot. However, he felt he must not leave everything to chance especially when the advert invited applicants from the public. He felt he was not good enough; otherwise, it could have been limited to the workers within the company. It pained him so much that he thought he needed help from a soothsayer. He contacted some of his friends whom he suspected indulged in such things and they were quite happy to have him in the game. And that was why he wasted no time to come over to Kayima to see Nonko, who encouraged him to stay for a night to get what he needed. He had no alternative but to be lodged in a room next to him. And it was while he was waiting that Sakayo's aunt came over to him. He was surprised to discover that she too came to seek Nonko's help. He wondered what sort of help she needed at her age, but he learnt everything in his room when she explained fully to the soothsayer what she wanted to achieve. It was quite a demonic affair and he was shocked. At a moment he almost decided to abandon his project if it was going to be a demonic affair. He made sure he recorded the entire message that the young boy received and the discussions that followed. He wanted to listen to the message in his quiet moment back in Koidu Town. But suddenly it occurred to him that Sakayo would need it because the whole plot was to have disunity in a home which he was managing. He felt good having recorded it with care without knowing how useful it would be to his friend. He sat down for many hours meditating on what to do to save Sakayo from the disaster that her aunt was planning. He felt he would never be a freeman if he did not inform him about the plot. He recalled quite clearly that he was a brilliant boy in school even though he was not properly fed. But despite his condition at home, he was charming, friendly and unassuming. He recalled that his fortune to travel abroad came when he saved the chief's son from falling from a tree. He was quite determined to call him as soon as he returned to Koidu Town. He recalled writing down in his notebook his cell phone number when he came to visit his parents some time ago. Early the next day Posua received half a pint of some concocted liquid which he must rub before appearing for the interview Board and he must continue to rub it to earn him fame and wealth. He examined the dirty liquid curiously and wondered what was in it that made it so powerful. He had already spent some money on it and no matter what it looked like he would use it. Besides, the colleagues who recommended Nonko said they got their monies worth out of the process. He looked at the bottle once more and shook it to see if there was something visible in it and special, but it looked like any normal dirty liquid. He then tried to open it but discontinued instantly because Nonko never said he should smell it, and he realized he was taking some unnecessary risk that was not called for. He then zipped open his bag and placed the bottle in a safer corner and tightened the stopper to avoid any spillage. He then closed the zip. At least he was happy that his concoction was not there to harm anybody but to ensure that he was favored and selected no matter what his performance was. He thought aloud for some time and realized that if somebody's performance was better than his and was not selected, would that not affect his life? He pondered as his analysis got more complex. He dropped the topic and tried to concentrate on the journey back to Koidu Town. He bid Nonko farewell and walked to the lorry park. He tried to make some calls but the battery was too low on his cell phone. He moved quickly down the hill and then spotted a vehicle by the market with a small crowd around it. He walked faster to secure a seat; otherwise he would have to wait for the next vehicle which normally left in the afternoon. He arrived and got a seat on the vehicle. In fact, it was the same vehicle that brought him. He checked to see where he sat the last time but it was occupied by a young beautiful lady. He noticed that he sat exactly where Nema sat and recalled that she was quiet and did not care what happened in the vehicle except when a deep pothole threw them apart when the vehicle drove into it. That was the only time she spoke to anybody in the vehicle. She appeared to be up to something sinister which he discovered without making any effort. Suddenly he noticed he was thinking too deeply. He turned around and spoke to passengers he found in the vehicle; especially the lady that sat in the seat which he occupied the other day. But there was too much noise around from a puncture exhaust pipe and a lively political discussion that was hotly debated without any winners. By the time his discussion with the lady became much more interesting, they were already in the lorry park in Koidu Town. Posua climbed down the vehicle, stretched his legs and walked around the vehicle to take the cell phone number of the lady, but she was already in a car moving towards Opera, the most popular entertainment centre in the city. He checked his mind quickly if he remembered her name but it was gone as well. He stood there monitoring the car's movement until it disappeared from his view. When he turned around, the apprentice was waiting to collect his transport fare. The issue of the lady and the car took his mind off the payment. He said sorry to the young man and took some money out of his pocket and paid. He counted the money and asked for an additional two thousand Leones which he said was due to fuel price hike the previous day. He paid and looked around and selected a bike rider out of many that made themselves available the moment the vehicle parked. He had a safe ride to his Sandoh Street residence where he dropped off after he had paid a non negotiable fare of one thousand Leones about (\$ 0.13). It was two days to the interview and he brought out of his drawer a series of documents relating to his job schedule and the code of conduct. He read through them carefully noting down important facts to remember. Throughout the weekend he read the documents until it was a few hours to the interview which was on a Monday morning. He dressed up early in one of his best suits after applying the concoctions on his face and arms and checked the dressing mirror to see whether everything was all right. He adjusted his collar and the neck tie and was satisfied with his looks. Then he went out and waved down a passing Motorbike which took him to the board room of Koidu Mining Company Limited. He was the first to arrive in the waiting room and sat directly opposite the air conditioner to cool down properly. Within a few minutes three other people joined him, two of them from his department. He became much more concerned with the female candidate who was lost in her thoughts, reflecting on a strange call on her mobile telephone asking her to see the Board chairman a day before the interview. She ignored the call and concentrated on the interview itself. While she waited in the waiting room she wished nobody would mention anything about the call that requested her to see the Board Chairman.

Looking at her from the corner of his eye, Posua wondered whether she was not using a concoction better than Nonko's. The two sat in the waiting room and glanced at each other suspiciously whilst they appeared to be concentrating on some other issues. Posua showed boldness and greeted her again and asked for her name. She tagged nervously at a strand of hair that fell on her face and announced that she was Kumba Kaye, a fresh university graduate in accounting. Posua's eyes shone with excitement and concentrated on her smallish size, tender age, admirable achievement, and beauty. The peace of the room was disturbed Suddenly, as rain came down harder, spattering noisily on the roof top, making further conversations impossible. He moved closer and gave her his background as a practicing accountant and read at Fourah Bay College which happened to be Kumba's alma materasw As far as the two men in the waiting room were concerned Posua rated himself higher than them, and with the concoctions on his face and arms, they did not stand any chance at all. But what if they too contacted other powerful soothsayers like Nonko that would pose a serious challenge to him. But he trusted his friends who recommended Nonko. They assured him that he was a man that never failed anybody. He built his confidence on that recommendation and remained calm until his name was announced to appear before the Board. He entered the Boardroom and the interview did not take as long as he expected. It was short and required a practical knowledge of basic accounting and people management. He felt he was up to the task and hoped for success. But he wondered why he was told to wait. Was there going to be a second interview? He could not understand what was going on and so he waited patiently for the others to be interviewed. Then the issue of gender equality came into his thoughts, a factor which, if taken into account, could hamper his chances. He was served breakfast as he waited in the waiting room meditating on the interview, the contestants and the magic of soothsayers as supporting elements for success. The first round of interviews ended and there were only two of them remaining in the waiting room; he and the lady. He agreed within himself ell. They discussed freely as if they knew each other before and forgot completely that they were there for an interview. Then suddenly Kumba's name was announced to appear before the Board again. But before she could move from her seat, he asked for her cell phone number and address. He noted them quickly in the notepad which he had with him. Alone in the waiting room his heart thudded for fear of losing the job to a very young lady which would make further advances impossible because if she got the job she would be his boss and supervisor at work. This will make life difficult and at home would he be a respected husband? As he delved into the issues mentally, Kumba's interview ended. She came out and realized that the instruction to see the Board Chairman before the interview was not brought up in her interview. Whatever could have been the motive, she was quite satisfied with her performance and she tried as much as possible to keep it out of her mind. She spoke briefly to Posua and left, waving back frantically at him. His eyes followed her until she disappeared around the corner. He wished the interview was delayed so that they could have some fruitful discussions. But with her cell phone number and address, something useful could be done. His chain of thought was broken when his name was called for the second interview. He was calmer than before and well prepared to tackle any tricky questions in order to win the job and build on the friendship with Kumba that began that very day. He was so moved by her looks and mannerisms that he could not but maintain her in his thoughts. He appeared in the Board room completely inattentive. He was asked to sit down twice but he happened to have heard it only the second time. He sat down and waited for questions. But no questions were asked; instead the Chairman of the Board spoke to him, in such a manner that gave him hope. He said that his performance was the best in all the areas tested. As a result he got the job. He thanked the six Board members and promised that he would continue to work hard to make his institution better. Back home that day joy was all over him. He lay down on his bed and listened to music from some gospel plates. He made a series of calls to some relatives and work mates and gave away the news about his success. He called Kumba twice but there was no answer. He sent her a text message and waited for a reply which did not come. Whilst waiting, he reflected on the interview. Did he get the job because of Nonko's concoction or was it due to his experience and hard work? He could not tell and remained with the two opinions until one day he accidentally broke the bottle and the concoction spilled out on the floor, filling the room with an offensive smell. He stood over it and reflected on its cost and potency, but it was gone. Reflecting on his adventure to Kayima he recalled that he had made a vow to talk to Sakayo about his findings about his Aunt Nema. He checked his note pad for his cell phone number. He went from page to page many times over until he found it. He searched his pen and noted down what he thought he should know and then dialed his numbers. The cell phone rang and then it was picked up. "My name is Posua, your classmate in UMC Primary School in Kayima. Can you recall the game "Think of any number" and the class competitions on Fridays"? He said and suddenly there was a shout of joy from the other end. "Good to hear from you my brother. I have asked Kaye, another classmate of ours where one could locate you but he too was not sure. I am happy that you kept my cell phone number. How are you and your wife if you have already got one"? He said heartily. "I am fine and still single, working for Koidu Mining Company.

I have just been promoted to the post of accountant. Have you got a partner yet?

I am sure you must have brought one from the United States of America", he said and laughed aloud.

"Congratulations Posua. This clearly shows that you have grown in your profession. Please keep it up. I am like you, without a partner yet. I am on the search and whenever I find one, you and other classmates will know", he said. "Good, I have called you because I have a piece of information for you which might be a bit disturbing but you need it. If you don't mind, I will forward it to your whatsApp", he indicated frankly. I don't mind at all Posua. "Go ahead", he assured him. And with a click on the cell phone, the recorded audio message was on Sakayo's whatsApp. He thanked him and promised to be in touch with him soon. Sakayo went quickly to his room and closed the door after him. He clicked once or twice on the cell phone and the whatsApp opened. He then clicked on the icon and listened. It was disturbing but he had to hear the whole story. He heard Nema's voice and her request to Nonko to bring enmity between his parents. What moved him more was the use of the demonic image and deploying an innocent boy to be part of the process. He came to the end of the recording and replayed it to understand it fully. At the end of the replay, he was quite convinced that Nema was speaking and meant evil for Betty in particular. He summed up courage and came out to the sitting room where his parents were waiting to hear how he spent his day. But instead of narrating the day's ordeals he sat close to them and urged them to listen keenly. He clicked on the icon and put it on loud speaker. Then suddenly they heard Nema's voice and her request to Nonko, followed by the discussions relating to the demonic image and the messages it gave out including burying a cock alive in the sitting room. Betty could not hold back her tears. She wept and held her head with both hands in torment. So many things ran through her mind; an untimely death for her and Sakayo or other forms of evil that might arrest his progress. "Entona, What have I done to Nema? Please tell me why she hates me and Sakayo so much? Tell me why she has brought demons into her house and specifically mentioned my name?" She asked, sobbing.

Entona was dumbfounded. He tried but could not find the words to address the situation. He went close to her and held her on both shoulders and spoke to her in low tones. The atmosphere was tense and nobody was in the right frame of mind to give a coherent speech.

Sakayo braved it up and asked his father for the way forward to what he had heard. He stood up and cleared his throat and chose his words carefully. "She has contacted a demon and has carried out its instructions in my own house. She has buried a cock alive in my sitting room together with my clothes, to bring disaster on the family. This wicked plot will be made known to herself and the entire town. I will never dwell in a house with demons. Although this is the only asset that I have, I don't mind losing it because I love my life. I don't expect any of you to dwell there either. With regards to Mary, she is mine and she too must be moved from there. Nema alone should stay there and bear the consequences of her demonic activities", he said. Entona's eyes became red and his face twisted in anger. He walked to his room briskly and returned within seconds and gave Sakayo a piece of paper on which was a cell phone number.

"Please call this number and let me speak to Chief Souï", he said in a confused state of mind. Sakayo dialed the number and gave the cell phone to him. He got the Chief and explained to him exactly what he heard on the clip and asked him to invite Nema to his house so that he could speak to her. The chief asked him to call back later. Nema got the news that Entona wanted to talk to her on the Chief's cell phone in the next few minutes. She received the message with joy, and believed that Entona was ready to return home. She felt Nonko's pronouncements were proving to be good. She went into her bedroom, changed her clothes and left for the Chief's compound. She walked faster than ever and arrived there within a short time. She walked through the corridor to the Chief's sitting room. She bowed down and greeted him but she was shocked that he was serious and did not joke with her as usual. Suddenly, he received a call on his cell phone, spoke briefly and handed the cell phone over to her. "Is that Nema? This is Entona on the line. I want you to listen carefully to what I am going to say to you today. We have evidence that you have contacted the soothsayer Nonko and his demons. They have asked you to bury a cock alive in my living room with some other materials including my clothes. You have dug a hole in my sitting room and buried a cock alive in that hole. You have done all that to ensure that Betty does not return home. I have decided not to enter that house as long as you are staying there with your demons", he proclaimed and then switched off the cell phone. Nema kept the cell phone on her ear hoping that Entona would continue talking. She was prepared to deny the allegations but the cell phone was completely silent. "Can you please give me back my cell phone if you are alright?" said the Chief.

She turned around and handed over the cell phone and walked out quickly. Her pressure rose and she could feel sweat trickling over her entire body. She arrived home without knowing it. Her mind was full of many issues; Mary, the revealed secret, the consequences on her and Mary, losing Entona, and the return of Betty. She decided that she would not be morally strong to face the consequences.

Chief Soui went on a short trip immediately after the Nema- Nonko affair. He went to a village which was outside the coverage of his cell phone company. He totally ignored his cell phone during the course of the visit, knowing quite well that he was missing so many calls, especially from Entona. He saw how tense he was when he last spoke to him. He spent a day in the village and returned to Kayima after settling a dispute between two families over a piece of farm land.

In Kayima he located his cell phone and put it on. A series of miss calls showed up and he checked to see those which needed an immediate response. It was whilst he was checking when a call registered. It was Entona on the line, and he did not waste any time but went straight to the issue. He explained in details the steps that he had taken to expel Nonko from Kayima and how he dug out what was buried in his sitting room with the help of the elders and youths. He furthered that Nema disappeared from the scene the next day to an unknown destination and that she was still missing from the town. However, he informed him that Hawa had consented to take care of Mary and he had agreed to provide food support to her until his return.

Entona came out of his bedroom from where he made the call and joined Betty in the kitchen. He explained to her exactly what the chief told him and they discussed the issue together and agreed that the chief had taken the right decisions and that he needed their support. His main concern was the security of Mary and her daily support which was adequately addressed at that moment. He was quite happy that the demonic elements were dug out from his sitting room which gave him confidence to return home within a short time. He sat down for a long time broodingover Nema's involvementwith a soothsayer and demons and how she disgraced herself in public. He shook his head in wonderment. Betty watched him whilst she shuttledbetween the house and the kitchen bringing items into the kitchen or taking them out into the store. "Nema is still your biggest problem. I know it is your wish to locate her as soon as possible. I understand that quite clearly and this is why I did not break your chainof thought until now. By the way, have you decided what to do to locate her? I am prepared to help you with my share of the money Sakayo gave us quite recently." She volunteered. "No, you are completely wrong this time. I am thinking about how we were separated from each other, because I still don't know how it happened. Perhaps you can tell me because I cannot remember having quarrels with you on any issue that was big enough to separate us. I am fairly convinced now that the food that Nema prepared for me could have been smeared with some liquid from the soothsayer to draw my mind away from you. I am just thinking aloud without any proofs." He explained, looking at her for a response. "Well, I don't know what happened. But most often you came home fed and failed to appreciate whatever I did at home. And above all, you did not open up to me, making me look like a stranger in my own house and you did not

163

show me any love," she said and burst into tears. He went quickly and held her close to himself and wiped her tears with his handkerchief and encouraged her to come into the sitting room with him. They walked into the room and sat very close to each other for the first time after many years of separation. "I want you to forgive me for all your sufferings. I was not by myself and so you could not have expected something better," he said and wiped his face often, apparently he too was crying. There was a deep silence for some time and then he broke it. "Now, with all the issue resolved, please, get yourself prepared for resettlement in Kayima with me. We cannot live here at the expense of Sakayo and I wish to ensure that my relationship with Nema is broken and can never be repaired because I cannot live with someone who operates with demons. I have loved you sincerely before and I want to assure you that I still love you because of your character of honesty and simplicity. I want you to have trust in me and continue to be patient with me," he said in a very serious tone. "well I don't have much to say but to listen to you again. I have waited for God's intervention in this matter for long, and if this is the time, then let it be so. But there is an urgent need for me to pass my first set of examinations with flying colors to be able to work in any of the hospitals in our community back home" she replied humbly. Entona grabbed her right hand and shook it until both of them burst into laughter. She withdrew her hand and ran into the kitchen to check whether the meat had cooked. From that day life became normal between Entona and Betty as she worked hard to complete her course at Connaught Hospital where she was doing extremely well in all subjects.

Nema became sick and went from one village to another seeking healing from herbalists and soothsayers. She ended up in Koidu town nearly after two years and sought healing in the Pentecostal Church called "The Saviour" with Philip Teh as the pastor in charge. In an exclusive interview on her illness, she confessed boldly her involvement with soothsayers and with occultists in a bid to secure Entona, her purported husband who was on the verge of abandoning her for Betty her arch rival. From that day, she became a member of the church and made herself available for daily prayers and the monthly deliverance sessions on the premises of the church. After many such sessions she became much better and had the feeling within herself that she was fully delivered from the oppressions of demons. She took part in the weekly Bible study program which was offered freely to all members. Her health returned to her gradually as her faith increased by hearing the word of God often. One day she called Entona on his mobile telephone and asked his permission to speak to Betty and it was granted. Betty held the phone to her ear and listened carefully. Nema went straight to the point and apologized for the mischievous things she did that affected her one way or the other and asked for forgiveness. She said that she has turned to a new page in her life. Calmly, Betty accepted the apology and forgave her for any wrong doings. When the telephoned went silent she turned to Entona for his reaction as the phone was on loud speaker. "God is great, Nema is indeed a changed person" he said and Betty agreed with him completely.

Nema later received Waters of Baptism in the Church and then joined the weekly soul winning outreach program in and out of Koidu town. A few years later, she became a recognized teacher of the word of God and counselor in teenage pregnancy, illicit abortions and occultism, from which many people benefited, including the boys and girls in the Church and outside it.

As her life returned to normal, she restarted her petty trading business which developed into a sizeable provisions shop in her new location which brought her more than enough income to solve her personal problems and contribute meaningfully to Mary's education. After many years of observation and background checks on suitors and with a lot of prayers, she got married to Aiah Sokena, a church member and the couple lived a quiet and happy life, with Mary receiving full support.

Chapter Ten

The Calabash Marriage

At the end of the day's work, Sakayo went straight to Kaye's house. His mind was still fully occupied with Kumba Kaye, Kaye's sister. She looked cool and calculated and above all beautiful. Each time he saw her, he was completely in love with her in his heart. But he was not going to rely absolutely on the factshe was his friend's sister. He decided to move independently to make his case even before he got the information. One evening he drove close to her house and parked in a location from where he could turn the vehicle with ease. He walked into the house and luckily found her alone. She was not surprised to see him so early judging from his stare, smiles and interest that he showed the other day. "Good evening", he said smiling. "Good evening", she replied. "Kaye is not yet at home. Do you intend waiting for him?" she asked. "Well, I have come to see you and not him. This is why I decided to come a bit earlier so that we can have enough time to ourselves", he said. "You are here to see me?" Are you sure it is me you want to see? Right, please have a seat, and here I am," she sat in the opposite chair and looked up at him boldly. "I, I have come to see you because I love you so much. I am speaking from the bottom of my heart and I mean what I am saying. And I want you to believe me. I have been planning my marriage since my return, but a key element has been absent, somebody I love", he explained, looking straight into her face. "When the first sentence of a suitor contains the word marriage, it does not make me feel happy. Why can't we discuss other issues first, understand each other better and then implement your so called plans later," she cautioned. "Madam, I am sorry but I always treat the subject matter of an issue first, being the foundation. And once we get the foundation right, the other issues will then help us to grow stronger and stronger", he tried to convince her. "There is rice with cassava leaves" she announced, trying to take his mind off his plans, and without waiting for a reply she went into the kitchen to prepare some food for him and to release some tension that had built up in her. She served the food and hoped that the discussion did not continue for too long because she expected her brother to be around at any time. "You have not made any comments. I take it that everything is ok", he asked with a broad smile. "You are talking about an issue that concerns committing one's life. Obviously, I need some time to look into that. But if I may ask, since your return have you not found anybody you love so much,"? She asked, looking straight at him. "I have not found anybody like you and I can prove this to you. Kaye is my proof because we have been up and down together ever since", he said. There was a knock on the door and she went over quickly and opened it. Before Kaye stepped in, Sakayo spoke in a loud voice from the dining table, "late comers do not enjoy hot food". "Oh boy, you are here. That's great! I will join you straight away on the table. Kumba, please bring additional food to the table. This man needs a lot of food to be as strong as I am", he said jokingly and then settled down beside him. "How long have you been here?" He asked and waited for his plate of rice rather than for the answer. Of course, the answer came. "I have been here for nearly 30 minutes, and I must confess that I have had the best of treatment," he admitted. "Keep coming and you shall be alright," he said. The two men conversed and argued as they ate, whilst Kumba pretended to be reading a book which was lying on her lap. When they finished eating she cleared the table and supplied a plate of ripe bananas and then went into her room to avoid the continuation of the love discussions in the presence of her brother. She prayed in her heart for Sakayo to go without referring to her for answers or comments. She had a lot of respect for her brother and would not like him to know about something that had not even taken off. Sakayo thanked Kumba and picked up his briefcase and indicated to Kaye that he was ready to go. He led the way followed by Kaye and then Kumba. "Please say hi to Mum and Dad", said Kaye when they were close to the vehicle and then he walked back to the house quickly as if he had forgotten to do something that exposed the house to some risk. Kumba was taken aback by his brother's move, leaving her face to face with Sakayo. She wanted to follow Kaye immediately, but without saying good bye would mean a lot. She knew if she said good bye he would ask some questions or ask for some favors to ensure that they went into a longer conversation. She was trapped and there was no way out of it. "Good bye", she said at last. "Can I have your cell phone number please?" He requested. She gave it quickly, waved and then ran back home. She looked from the corner of her eye and found him staring at her as she ran back home. But finally he started the vehicle and left the premises. When she was back in the house she went straight into her room ashamed and afraid of her brother. She did not come out even for their usual story telling Programme which linked them directly to their history and culture which both of them enjoyed. Kaye realized that she was afraid and then called her immediately and asked why she went to bed too early. She explained that she was tired and feeling sleepy. After her explanation which was not convincing, he spoke to her frankly on the issue. "You have been a good lady ever since in both your academic and domestic life. I am actually very proud of you as a sister and I am quite prepared to support you in anything that will make you happy. I don't know what may have happened between you and Sakayo. But if he says he loves you, he means it and if he promises to marry you, he will do it. And if he marries you, then you have a good husband indeed. We became friends from primary school and he is always stable in character and honest in every deal. Mistakes may occur along the line but with your character and his, it is always easy to find a solution. Don't hesitate and don't hide anything from me. I will be a happy man too if he marries you, being almost a brother to me", he lectured her. "Thank you brother," she said and asked if she could serve him tea. "Oh, I was just about to ask for it. Please add some lime to it and just a cube of sugar", he requested and moved to the dining table quite satisfied that he had done justice to his conscience.

Sakayo arrived home and found his parents eating happily from the same plate. He greeted them and enquired about his father's health even though he knew quite well that he had recovered completely. He confirmed that he was well and eating very well. He went into his bedroom and thanked God for His marvelous work of unity in the life of his parents. When he came out after some time he found them sitting close to each other and ready with a piece of information for him. Entona then explained in full what had happened in Kayima in the last two weeks. He confessed openly that he had wronged Betty and the reason for his inconsiderate behavior could be partly explained by Nema's relationship with a demonic soothsayer. He said that once the demonic objects have been removed from the house and the Church passed the night there praying, they had agreed to go back and get on with their lives and take care of Mary. He said that as far as he was concerned Nema was out of the equation because she used demons to achieve her goals contrary to his faith in hard work. He confirmed that his relationship with Nema ended the moment it was proved that she got involved with demons to ensure that Betty stayed out of the home permanently. Sakayo received the news like a dream. He was already planning to have another house built in Kayima because he had heard his father saying that he would never live with demons. He was amazed at the way things worked out for him. Moreover Kumba was good news to him and would be good news to his parents as well. And above all, the unity between his parents would be good news to everybody in Kayima. He went to bed that night in a happy mood and slept like a baby.

Posua woke up with pain in his right leg. Coming home from work the commercial Motor Bike ran into another at a junction and he fell and hit his right leg on a rock. Whilst he was struggling with the pain both riders disappeared quickly from the scene. He was helped to sit on another Motor Bike which took him safely home in the evening. The pain got worse the next morning and he called his office immediately and obtained permission to see the doctor at the Koidu Government Hospital. He arrived at the Hospital and sat on one of the chairs in the waiting room, amidst several other patients who had come earlier than him. Looking around the room he recognized the young boy he saw in Nonko's house in Kayima. "Are you the one I saw in Kayima in Nonko's house?" he asked. Saafea stared at him for long and then nodded his head, indicating that he was the one. "Do you know him?" asked Biango who accompanied Saafea to the hospital. "Yes", said Posua. "I went to see Nonko and whilst I was there a certain lady brought him into the house. I recognized him as soon as I sat here on this chair. "Is Nonko in Kayima?" he asked. "He has been expelled from there after the entire township proved that he was putting demonic spell on people. We dug out from a certain house a dead cock that was buried alive and other items, including a man's clothes", he explained. Posua became stiff and his blood ran faster in his veins. He could feel it on his arms and in his head. But he pretended to be calm and continued to ask more questions. "Please, can you tell me the family that was affected directly?" he asked again trying to know whether it was Sakayo's aunt that was involved. "It was Entona's wife that was involved. And as I speak to you, she is moving from one town to another, under demonic oppression. Nobody has succeeded in containing her, not even her parents in her home town, Penduma", he explained. "Did you say you saw this boy in Nonko's house?" asked Biango. "Yes, he was with Aunty Nema and they were right Inside Nonko's bedroom," he explained. Biango then told Posua that the boy in question, Saafea was collapsing in school very often, and each time he told his teachers that he saw a devil. Many attempts were made to treat him by applying various medicines which did not improve his condition. It was further suggested that he did not like Kayima School and so he pretended to have seen a devil, so that he could be transferred to another school. And indeed he was transferred to Koidu United Methodist Church School. Out there too, he continued to collapse in class from time to time, confessing to have seen devils. Posua received the news with a shock. He recalled quite clearly that the concocted liquid in the bottle which he had received from Nonko and which he had applied on his arms and on his entire body was demonic. Fear gripped his body and sweat started running down his face. If Nema was under demonic oppression after obeying his instructions, then it was just a matter of time for him to behave in a similar manner, he thought. He had just learnt that the little boy who received the messages was sick, collapsing and claiming to have seen devils. Was he going to escape demonic attack being one of them that received objects from him? He could not see any escape route as far as demonic attacks were concerned. He stopped any further mental analysis of the issue and received treatment for his aching leg and left the hospital on a Motorbike because he needed to rest properly for his leg to heal quickly. He arrived home in a confused mind. He sorted the clothes that he wore during the interview and some others which he wore after applying the liquid to his arms and face. He placed all of them in a bucket and took them to the garden at the back of the house. He set fire to them and ensured that they were burnt to ashes. He did not like to be oppressed by demons and decided to take all necessary precaution to forestall any attack. He came back into his room and removed the center table and chairs and cleaned the floor thoroughly. He recalled that the bottle containing the concocted liquid broke exactly in the centre of the room spilling the liquid on the floor. He had cleaned the floor but not as thoroughly as he would have done with soap and brush. Additionally, he laundered his beddings and dried them properly. In the evening he went to a nearby church where a night service was going on. He attended the service and at the end he met the Pastor and explained exactly what had happened between him and Nonko. He was prayed for and sent home with some scriptures which he had to memorize and recite whenever he felt his life was in danger. He came back home very satisfied that the prayers would counter any demonic oppression that might affect him. He relaxed on his bed and tried to concentrate on other issues other than the liquid and its effects. Then suddenly he recalled that he had made several calls to Kumba but did not go through. He took his cell phone and tried her again. The cell phone rang and he sat up quickly to talk to her. "Hi Kumba, it's me Posua from Koidu Mining Company, your interview mate for the post of Accountant. Do you remember me?" he asked and waited.

"Yes, I remember you very well. Congratulations. I learnt that you got the job", she said. "Thank you very much. I have tried to get to you but your cell phone was not on except today. How are you?" he asked with interest. "Sorry about that Posua. My cell phone was stolen shortly after I took the interview in Koidu town. It was only a few days ago that I got a new cell phone and regained my Sim Card. Sorry about that!" she said frankly. "When are you coming back to Koidu town? And if you are not coming so soon, can I pay you a visit out there?" he requested. "Thank you very much for showing such an interest in me. But if I may ask what would be the subject of the visit?" she asked. "Well, let me speak the truth which is coming from the bottom of my heart. I want you to be my life partner. I don't have any doubt in my mind that you are the right person for me", he said and waited for an answer. But no answer came. "Hello, are you on line", he asked anxiously. "Yes, I am. I appreciate you very much. I really think that you are a good guy, but I am sorry to say that I am already engaged and I am fully committed to it," she said. "Oh my God, Who is that lucky fellow?" he asked. "Posua, don't try to venture into that. Just accept that I am not available for your request but available as a friend", she said and waited for his reaction. "Does it actually matter if I know the person?" He asked anxiously. "If you don't mind I will tell you. He is called Sakayo." The name Sakayo rang a bell. He knew exactly who she was taking about, his classmate and one he refused to share his food with a long time ago. "Thank you very much. Goodbye and good luck in all your endeavors", he said and waited for some more reactions but Kumba was no longer online. He reviewed his bold attempt and blamed himself for being too much in haste. He felt that his request ought to have been made a month earlier, after the first encounter. He felt he had messed it up completely. Could he make another trial, he pondered. Posua toyed with various approaches that could remedy the situation as he lay on his bed. But before he could decide on the right approach, he fell asleep.

Biango and Saafea returned home after the doctor failed to see any sickness associated with Saaffea's frequent visual disturbances and falls. From the information he got from Posua, he took him aside and asked him what he was doing in Nonko's house. He looked on sheepishly as if he did not understand the question. In fact, he understood it quite well but when he recalled the punishment for disclosing the secret he refused to talk.

He pressured him for months trying to find out exactly what he did so that he could find a solution to his illness. One day he explained to him exactly what he did in Nonko's house. It amounted to contacting a demon, the reason for his frequent attacks. For many months Biango tried to treat him through various mediums but without any success. He could not continue his schooling due to the stigma and financial difficulties and ended up in a village called Gbande-Kordu, where an herbalist treated him. The treatment took the form of a blanket over his head with a hot pot of herbs between his legs, from which his eyes received vapors from the herbs. Indeed he stopped seeing the demons and stopped collapsing but the color of his eyes gradually became blood shot as he continued the treatment. As he grew up he eventually lost his eye sight and remained in the village. His blindness did not stop all his normal activities. He was able to fetch fire wood and went into any house he wanted to because he knew the position of each house in the village, and knew every person by his voice. He was fond of a puppy which he named Manne, which meant light. He fed the puppy out of whatever food supplement he got from the herbalist and other sympathizers, the main support coming from Biango who initially operated his Motorbike between Kayima and Koidu town, but moved over to Koidu where he did better business. The opportunity of short distance hires with double or triple the normal charge was plentiful. Besides, Koidu had better Motorbike mechanics and services and cheaper spare parts than any of the towns and villages in Sandoh chiefdom. When he moved over to Koidu his Motorbike became almost like a brand new one after servicing it and replacing some of the old parts. The renovation on the

Motorbike gave him a renewed zeal to venture out to distant towns on hire which earned him some good sum of money. He was further encouraged by his earnings to build himself a house in Gbande- Kordu, his home town and to maintain his oil palm plantations out there. When his Motorbike broke down eventually after some years of active work, he decided to move over to Gbande- Kordu to harvest his plantations which had yielded their first fruits. His presence out there brought happiness to Saafea being his main support base. They were not relatives by blood but Biango knew his parents very well and knew exactly what happened to them, the main reason why he was sympathetic with him. Saafea proved to be very useful to the town, providing day watch for them with the help of Manne when the farmers were out in the field during the day.

Sakayo and Kumba called each other every moment of the day, and it went beyond calls to frequent visits. They loved each other and longed to be together as husband and wife. One evening he brought Kumba home, and that was her first visit ever. They walked into the sitting room and found his parents watching a programme on the television. He reduced the volume of the TV and then introduced Kumba as their daughter in-law to be. Both parents got up and embraced her warmly and assured her of their support and encouraged her to continue to be a good woman. "This is your house. Try not to be a stranger here. Please make yourself comfortable," Sakayo said and sat close to her. Entona and Betty were full of admiration for Kumba. Betty was so moved that she went and sat close to her and engaged her with questions about her parents, brothers and sisters and about other issues. It was all joy and laughter in the house that evening, and to sustain it Sakayo got up and took cold drinks from the fridge and served everybody starting with Kumba and then his parents. The service continued through out the evening until late at night. Kumba drew Sakayo's attention to the time and indicated that she had stayed longer than it was expected. Sakayo took his cell phone and called Kaye and explained to him that Kumba was having a good time with his parents the reason why she was late and promised to take her home immediately after dinner. And indeed he informed his parents immediately that she was ready to leave them with a promise that she would be seeing them once every week. She hadn't enough time to be with them for dinner so she took her package home. Before she left, Betty hugged her and held her hand as they walked towards the vehicle which was parked outside the garage. When she got on board the vehicle, she looked out and found Betty still waiting to see that the vehicle took off and everything was OK. She liked Kumba so much that she wished Sakayo would marry her without much delay. The only thing occupying her mind at that moment was marriage. She did not want any obstacles that would prevent Sakayo from marrying her and she wished the marriage was the next day. When the vehicle started, she moved closer to see how they related to each other, and she was quite satisfied because she found them smiling at each other. Suddenly, the vehicle moved speedily and when he watched he saw his mother still staring at the vehicle. Betty smiled to herself when she realized that they noticed her curiosity and moved to avoid her watchful eyes. "Sakayo, your mother mumbled some words in my ear. Guess what she said to me", she asked. "I cannot tell you precisely all that she might have said to you, but I can tell you one key word in her statement, that is, marriage. She wants it now and not later. And I quite agree with her", he said. "You told me that you love me from your heart. In case there is a change of mind, what security do I have", she asked. Sakayo stopped the vehicle at a convenient point on the road. He turned round and stared at her in a very strange way. "I love you with all my heart which will never change until heartless death do us part. I mean exactly what I have said to you, please trust me", he said and held her two hands into his and encouraged her to look into his eyes. They giggled until they burst into laughter and tears of joy ran down their cheeks. It was like a vow that they took to be faithful to each other for ever. Sakayo dropped her at her residence and said goodbye many times without moving away. It was only when Kaye came out that he said his final goodbye hastily and moved away. Kumba went into her bedroom and tried to assess whether she made any progress with him. She felt good because she got more assurance at a moment when he was thoughtful and in a serious mood. As she was about to relax on her bed, her cell phone rang. "Honey, how are you? I just want you to know that I have arrived safely home," he said. "That is good. I was also planning to call you but I thought you were still driving. "Thank you for updating me. Have a blessed night with lots of love", she said. "Good night", he replied, realizing that she would not like to disturb Kaye with a lot of conversation at odd hours. He went to bed and the next moment he was fast asleep.

Entona received a call from Chief Soui relating to three important issues; that Nema had never been seen or heard of anywhere; Mary was looking forward to seeing him, and indicated also that his job would not be guaranteed when his sick leave had expired long since and he was expected to show up soon to take up his position to ease some constraints on the chiefdom Administration. He did not mince his words at all. He was quite aware that he had received good medical attention and was quite well. He thought he should have called to explain that he was well and that he was on his way but he never made such calls even though they were in contact with each other. His mind was made up that if he did show up in the coming days his job would be advertised.

Entona was quite aware about the Chief's concern and without wasting time he engaged Betty on the issue. The call coincided with Betty's final examinations in her nursing course. She worked on the subjects with all seriousness to ensure that she was successful at the end. Each morning Sakayo dropped her at Connaught Hospital and she stayed there until in the afternoon. She would then go to the market and buy the cooking items for the day. That was the way she managed the home until Entona's arrival. When Entona contacted her on the issue of returning home, she was in agreement with him and both of them were prepared to confront Sakayo immediately about their desire to return home. It was a concerted effort that was intended to please him and push him to send them away quickly. Sakayo returned home in the evening and found them sitting quietly around the table. He sensed something was seriously wrong. He wished it had nothing to do with Kumba and his plans for her. He went into his bedroom and waited to be told what happened. He waited there for quite some time but he was not told anything. Then he came out of the bedroom eager for information and sat on a chair by the dining table. Entona then made known to him the content of the messages that he got from Chief Soui and indicated to him that he and Betty had agreed to go back home and continue their life out there. Internally, Sakayo was pleased that it had nothing to do with his plans to marry Kumba. He sat down for some time analyzing the financial implications. He agreed with them to make the trip but only after his marriage arrangements. He informed them that their presence was crucially important for the accomplishment of the marriage arrangements and promised to fund their trip immediately after his wedding. They sat down together and worked out the dates and the people to be invited both in Freetown and in the provinces. A week later several people were informed of the date and venue for the occasion. It was obviously at Kaye's residence. Telephone calls were made across the country to people closely related either to Sakayo or to Kaye, including friends. Sakayo also made calls to the Andersons and to some of his friends abroad informing them that he was ready to marry one Kumba Kaye, a university graduate in accounting and his best friend's sister. They congratulated in advance and wished him well in all his endeavors.

Within two weeks everything that concerned the marriage was arranged. The lodge for the visitors was arranged by the two families. Kaye's aunt Bondu and Chief Soui arrived in Freetown and were lodged with Kaye. Several other visitors came for the marriage and lodged elsewhere in the city with relatives or with friends. The work mates of both Kaye and Sakayo were quite prepared. They got together and came up with a handsome contribution towards the marriage which went a long way in acquiring some of the items that Sakayo was required to buy. On the D-day, the delegation to meet

Kaye's family assembled in Sakayo's sitting room. They comprised some elderly family members in Freetown and from the provinces led by Entona and Betty. They had made several calls to ensure that the key stakeholders were present and ready to receive them. Of course, Kaye had made all the necessary arrangements, including hiring of cooks to prepare special dishes, hiring of Kono musicians with drums and sheburehs and hiring of a musical set with a variety of songs in English and in the National Languages. He was quite prepared. In fact, his worry was whether Sakayo would not make mistakes that may delay the process. Sakayo and Kumba also bought a lot of assorted drinks and transported them to Kaye's house. Indeed, both sides were ready and everything moved very fast as if the arrangement had begun a year ago. Perhaps, the strong bond of friendship between the two made the process a lot easier. They were great friends indeed but one personality was still absent. It was Yei Tomossi, Kaye's fiancé studying nursing at the Segbwema Hospital. She was a final year student. She got married to Kaye when she had just completed fifth form at the Ahmaddiyya secondary in school in Bo town some years ago. Before she got married, she stayed with Sergeant Aiah Tomossi at Gondama Military Barracks from where she attended school in Bo. She had to continue her studies on the advice and support of her husband which was indeed a very courageous decision. But the four years of waiting proved very difficult for both parties in terms of cost and the long distance between them. But she had barely two months to the completion of the final examinations. Kaye kept calling on her cell phone to know exactly where she was between Segbwema and Freetown. She had left very early but she had to go through many check points where she had to chlorinate her hands as many times as there were check points, together with temperature checks. That took a lot of her time and that caused Kaye a lot of worries because some of the calls that he made did not go through since she was outside the coverage of the cell company. Kaye's next call found her at Hastings, and that brought some happiness and relief to him. Her absence could have been interpreted negatively by family members who did not know that she was a student. She used taxis and Motorbikes to ensure that she was not late for the key elements of the marriage. She found joy and happiness at home and she took a central position in all the arrangement to ensure that every assignment was accomplished within the required time. It was not a strange thing to her to organize big parties. A year ago when she was on vacation, she organized a big party on her husband's 30th birthday celebration. It went well and they had a good time.

The delegation to meet Kaye took off early in the afternoon to ensure that the program was conducted in the day light. A young girl carried the calabash on her head wrapped in white. She led the way to the door which was locked according to the Kono tradition. The spokesman on the side of Sakayo was Entona himself being someone who understood the Kono tradition well enough. He knocked the door and said that he was a good stranger with gifts for the family. The spokesman on the side of Kaye, Chief Soui argued that it was late and risky to open the door to a stranger whose intentions he did not know. They argued for quite some time displaying their knowledge in their own tradition, and then the door was opened. The young girl led the way into the house where a whole section of the room was reserved for the visiting team. Entona then brought out many sealed envelopes as gifts containing various sums of money according to the positions in the family. The parents of the bride had more, next the aunts, the uncles, brothers, sisters, nephews, nieces, and other relatives staying in the house with the bride. Then the Pastor, the Imam of the area, chiefs and neighbors. A few envelopes without names were reserved for people that were missed out or for institutions or procedures and processes that were not correct. Chief Soui thanked his counterpart and his team and showered praises on them for the gifts. He assured him and his team that he was quite prepared to entertain them for as long as they were guests in Kaye's house. "A frog does not hop in the day without a cause; either a snake is chasing it or it is chasing its own prey", he said looking sarcastically at Entona. "A snake that does not know its prey ends up in frustration. Once upon a time, a crab was on the sand along a small river. A snake saw it from a tree top and descended quietly and set an ambush for it. The crab fell into the ambush and there was a fight. The crab held the head of the snake with its two large claws, and then used each of its ten legs to hold fast some portions of its long body. The snake struggled to free itself from its grips but it could not, and then shouted in pain. "Help, Help. They have ganged on me", said the snake, failing to realize that it was battling with a single crab. That snake did not know its prey well enough, and that is why it suffered at the end," he explained to the curious crowd. Entona responded "We are different. We know what we want and we are quite confident that we understand her just like she understands us. To cut matters short, he declared, we are here for a beautiful "flower" that we saw in the house sometime ago", declared Entona as the crowd listened keenly to capture the highlights. "Did you say you saw a "flower" in my house? How could you do that without coming over there? And if you came there illicitly, then you have broken the rules of engagement and this leads us to the realm of fines,"Chief Soui charged and got applause from the elders. Entona then passed over one of the reserved envelopes to the elders to settle the fine after pleading guilty. "You have just told me that you saw a "flower" in my house. Tell me something concrete about what you saw to guide my judgment" the chief continued, smiling. "Yes, I saw a beautiful 'flower', fair, slender, and tall with curly hair", he emphasized. "Well, I have many "flowers" in this house and your description is not adequate enough to lead me to any particular one", Chief Soui then turned to the crowd to know whether he was on the correct path, and there was a thunderous clap of hands. "Do you wish to see your "flower", in case we agree that you can see her?" he asked. "Oh yes, I saw a flower and this is why I am here in a grand style not like a beggar. I think I am well off to see who I want to see. I am quite prepared for that," said Entona demonstrating confidence and courage. "Good", his opposite number said and turned to a group of ladies assigned to the "flowers" and instructed them to bring in the "flowers" one after the other until the right 'flower' was identified. The ladies in charge of the "flowers" moved swiftly and covered the head of one extra bride and brought her in majestically from the room where Kumba and the extra brides waited. They sang and danced, whilst others imitated the sound of a car's horn to imply that they were driving her to the scene. The young bride sat right in the centre of the crowd and

Entona came forward to uncover her head but he was stopped immediately. "You have to do something before you can touch her", said one of the ladies. Entona walk back to his hand bag and brought out a reserved sealed envelope and handed it over to the lady, and then he was allowed to uncover her head. But unfortunately, it was not the bride he was looking for. "Please bring up my bride" he said. "How can your bride be brought without paying the transport fare for the one on the stage to return home", shouted the crowd. Entona put his hand into his pocket, pull out some money and gave it out as transport fare for the return of the rejected bride. All extra brides went through the same procedure and Entona bore the brunt of the financial cost. Whilst the brides were shown to the crowd, Sakayo and his friends were in a room in another house close to Kaye's. Kono tradition only allowed him into the ceremony when the formalities were almost complete. That was why an emissary kept moving in and out to provide details on how far they had gone with the ceremony. When it was time for the actual bride to be brought out, the caretaker ladies then created a scene to have some more money, at a time when everybody was anxious to see the bride. They said that their vehicle hadn't enough fuel, for which they received some money but they also came back and said that they had a breakdown on the way and they needed some money to pay the mechanics. They received enough money to encourage them to bring out the bride. Nobody could do it except them. Therefore money had to be spent or appeals had to be made for the sake of time. That was what moved them to bring out the real bride, Kumba. When the bride was brought out and her head uncovered to reveal it was she, there was singing and dancing. The drums sounded, the 'Sheburehs' shook and men and women danced. That was the crucial point in the ceremony. If the bride was not found then there could be no marriage. There was a time when a certain parent wanted to betroth her daughter to a certain rich man against her wish. The calabash was brought but the bride was not found, and there was no marriage, much to the disappointment of the visitors. Kumba was found and that was why the people were joyful and danced as if that was their last. When Chief Soui got to address the crowd the singing and dancing stopped immediately for the continuation of the ceremony. "If this is your 'flower' then let us know why you are here", he told Entona, who got up and made signs to his delegation. The young girl with the wrapped calabash got up and walked towards Kumba. That was yet another crucial point. If she did not want to be married but she could not escape from her parents, then she could refuse to accept the calabash. The young lady walked towards her, all eyes on her. The calabash was presented to her and she received it without any hesitation. The drums and sheburehs sounded and made their loudest noises, inviting the crowd to dance and enjoy themselves. Kumba, full of smiles looked around and located her aunt, Bondu close to Kaye. She moved to them, kneeled down and handed the calabash to her. She blessed her and wished her many children in her marriage and the necessary support for their upbringing. She passed on the calabash to Kaye who represented his late father. Kaye then selected some elderly women and gave them the calabash which they took into one of the rooms to know what it contained. They settled down and took their time and opened it and checked the items in it. They found a sum of one million

Leones, two wrappers of different colors of clothes, two reams of thread, a bundle of needles, fifty Kola nuts, some alligator pepper, a pair of rings, and a Bible. They took note of everything and consulted with Kaye and relatives and then came out and asked for some explanations for the exceptional items found in the calabash. Entona got on his feet again and said that everything that was in the calabash was deliberately put there. The kola nuts were a symbol of peace to the family; the needles and threads were to empower the woman to sew her husband's clothes whenever they were torn; the alligator pepper was there to warn the couple that disputes may arise but the kola nuts would provide the required peace; the rings were a symbol of love for the couple and the Bible provided the overall reference point for all their problems. And finally, the two wrappers were for the parents of the bride. It was at that point that food and drinks were served whilst music played in the background. Camera men stood at strategic positions and captured all highlights, especially the point of receiving of the calabash. Suddenly, an uncle to Kumba came out and stopped the music and took a central stage in the whole affair. He informed the crowd that he was the rightful husband of Kumba and he was there to take her away. He presented the sum of thirty thousand Leones to the elders to claim his wife. Uncles were considered by tradition to be the symbolic husbands of their nieces and for that reason tradition recognized his claim and factored it in the program. Entona reacted promptly by producing an equal sum to be offered to the uncle to give up his claims over the bride. He conceded and earned himself Thirty Thousand Leones. In another swift move Entona brought out another Ten Thousand Leones and blocked any other uncle who may be planning to make claims on Kumba onto the end of the occasion, and the elders managing the process endorsed the preemptive strike. They said he should have done that early to avoid that expenditure. Then Sakayo and his group entered into the room majestically and the crowd welcomed them with a big clap of hands whilst the drums and sheburehs played some traditional music to welcome them. It was all laughter and joy, singing and dancing when Sakayo took his position on the chair next to Kumba. They were full of smiles as they posed for the camera. Finally, a pastor was called upon to administer the rings and to introduce the Bible. That was yet another highlight. The camera men took vantage positions and camera lights flashed from left to right. The Pastor came to the stage and asked everyone to stand up and close their eyes before the Almighty God. He prayed generally and then prayed for the couple and administered the rings after declaring them husband and wife. He presented the Bible to Kumba and said that the solutions to all their problems would be found therein and encouraged them to consult it on a daily basis. Then the all night jubilation started with an incessant flow of food and drinks. Teenage boys and girls from the neighborhood ate to their satisfaction and engaged themselves in gathering empty bottles, spoons or cups to which they appeared to be very committed. As it went past midnight, the house became virtually empty of the visitors with the exception of the bride and groom, the parents and a few relatives who were lodging with Kaye. Kumba went into her room and took a few essential things that she would need in her new home. Sakayo joined her in the room and helped bring out the suitcase and a travelling bag. Whilst Sakayo shuttled in and out of the room, bringing out items, Kumba stood quietly at the door post and sobbed when Kaye bid her farewell. It was a difficult moment because she was like a daughter to him. He had taken her from their parents at a tender age and provided all the support she needed, both at home and in school. She got to know her mother better when her father died a few years ago. That was the first time he took her along to see her mother nearly after fifteen years. She knew her parents but the early separation made them like strangers to her. It was Kaye who did everything for her and made her what she was. As she stood at the door sobbing, aunt Bondu took notice of her and came closer. She too could not hold back her tears. She recalled that she never had the opportunity to live with Kumba and give her the love that she deserved, being the only daughter of her late sister. She stayed with her for about one year when Kaye took her to Freetown. He always kept her in Freetown for fear that she might be initiated into the Bondo Secret Society any time she went to stay with aunt Bondu and other relatives. That was why she stayed in Freetown all the time. Kaye too, looking at them, became emotional and used his handkerchief to wipe his face often. Sakayo was caught in the middle of the emotional outpourings, but stayed close to his wife, touching her and speaking into her ears, and wiping away her tears. Sakayo got the luggage into the vehicle and drove through the thick of the night, with Kumba in the front seat and Entona and Betty in the passenger seat. They were happy but completely tired. When they arrived home, Sakayo parked the vehicle into the garage and left it there with the suitcase and other items and held onto his wife who had not fully recovered from the shock of the parting. But the moment they entered their room there was joy and laughter once more. The next day Kaye woke up and reflected on the marriage and felt it was the right thing that happened to Kumba, to have his best friend as her husband. He was in deep thought 1 when suddenly he felt a hand on his head. It was Yei's hand followed by a question. "Why are you so thoughtful?" she asked. "I am thinking about your short stay which is not good for me especially now that Kumba is going away" he explained. "No, you should enjoy my presence and stop thinking about something in the future. I have only a few months more in that school and you will have me continuously. I know it has been difficult for both of us, but we decided it that way", she explained. "Honestly, I was reflecting on Kumba's successful marriage which has made all of us happy. But you have said the right thing. I need your continuous presence and that will make me a happy man, especially now that Kumba is gone", he explained. Satisfied with the explanation she got up and went into the kitchen to prepare breakfast. She came to Freetown the day before the wedding ceremony and she was the lead person for the entertainment of the guests. She was feeling a little tired because she went to bed very late but she felt she was doing her duty and tried to be strong. Breakfast was ready within a short time and the service was to all who lodged in the house for the occasion, including Chief Soui and Kumba's aunt, Bondu. Kaye went into his bedroom and asked Yei to come. When they were both sitting on the bed he spoke to her softly. "I have something to tell you which I hid from you for a long time", he said smiling. "I hope you are not going to tell me you made somebody pregnant due to my long absence, because this will destroy the union", she said, a

191

bit tensed. "No, far from it, it is always good news with me. I made an agreement with a car dealer long ago, wherein a reasonable chunk of my salary has been paid monthly for an automatic Pathfinder Jeep. Obviously, we need one especially now", he said. She was contrite smiling. "I am sorry honey. Indeed this is good news. You know that I trust and have confidence in you," she said smiling. "Thank you very much. Continue to have confidence in me until we get children; we need just four: Saa, Tamba, Sia and Kumba, two boys and two girls. Now, I am going to the Bank to have the car out today. I need to drive you and our guests around town, especially Chief Soui and my mother, who do not know how big this city is," he held her hand and squeezed it to laughter. Betty got up early in the morning and went into the kitchen to prepare breakfast. It was her habit to get up early and look around for some pieces of work to do. Besides, for her that morning was special with a long awaited daughter in law secured within the extended family network, for which she was very grateful. She would not mind to continue with the cooking to give her enough time to enjoy her marriage. She got the breakfast on the table and put a bucket full of hot water in the bath room for the couple. She loved Kumba so much that she could do anything for her. She tapped on the door and Sakayo answered inside. "There is hot water in the bathroom and breakfast is ready", she said and moved away. Kumba, who sat close to Sakayo came out thanked and assured her mother- in- law that she was there to take up her full responsibility in the home. She promised her that she would do everything possible to satisfy her husband. Kaye came back home when lunch was ready. He brought a blue Jeep which looked good in and out.

Sakayo and the rest of the household came out to appreciate it and were full of admiration for it. Yei climbed into the car smiling and sat in the passenger seat. She opened the locker and fiddled with the manual that she found in there. She loved the car and appreciated her husband's effort in securing it. After lunch Kaye drove them to the National Stadium and then to the Parliament building. From there they went as far as Waterloo through Hill Station and Regent and returned to Freetown through Calaba Town, Wellington, and Kissy Road and ending up at PZ through Sani Abacha Street. Chief Soui and Bondu could not believe their eyes. They said that nobody could understand the city as well as they understood their towns like Kayima or even Koidu town. They returned home in the comfort of the new car, fully satisfied about what they learnt about the city. Also, in the evening he drove them to Sakayo's house. The hosts were taken by surprise when they saw the car because they never knew Kaye had a vehicle, although Sakayo had an idea about the venture. Again, all the people in Sakayo's house came out and thanked Kaye for the car. It was indeed a lovely one. Kumba was so amazed when she learnt that the car belonged to her brother. She did not know he was saving to purchase it. Perhaps that was why he had a strict policy on expenditure and did not spend his money foolishly. The two families sat together and discussed quite a broad range of issues including the resettlement of Betty and Entona and the return of the other guests. They agreed on a date and the distribution of the passengers for the two cars. Kaye and Yei agreed to carry Chief Soui and Bondu. Obviously, Sakayo would carry his parents and the journey was within three days. Sakayo gave enough money to Kumba to shop for his parents; and each day she went out with them and brought some items. They bought virtually everything that was scarce in the village setting, including matches, magi sauce, good spoons, good dresses, drinking buckets, and the like. If Sakayo's car hadn't got a carrier it would have been difficult to take their goods on a single trip.

Yei too received some money from Kaye to shop for his aunt and to buy a big gown for the Chief which he appreciated very much. The end of the three days came very quickly. The day before the departure, Kaye and Yei came over and sat with Sakayo to conclude arrangements on the fuel and the time of leaving. They agreed on 6 am which meant that the ladies had to get up earlier than usual to prepare some food for the journey. The point of convergence was Shell, a popular park for all provincial bound vehicles and a location where travelers normally bought their final items from petty traders who were always there in large numbers. Pick pockets took advantage of the large crowd to steal cell phones from unsuspecting passengers as they went about looking for the required items. Sakayo packed and reviewed the packing making some adjustments. The items were too many but each item was valued and could not be left behind. It was getting to 6 am and Entona and Betty were ready and food was ready. They sat at the dining table and ate what they could and climbed into the car for the journey.

The streets were virtually empty, so Sakayo drove to Shell without any traffic obstructions and found Kaye and others waiting. Both teams bought some loaves of bread and half a dozen tins of sardine each. The journey began in earnest with Kaye leading the way, being more familiar with the road networks to the provinces. He knew quite well that it would be a smooth drive up to Matotoka but beyond that point it was difficult to move at 64km per hour because of the potholes and the construction work on the road. That was why Kaye sped on the good road, forcing Sakayo to do the same to gain enough time for the bad road. Kaye maintained his lead but he realized he had gone too far ahead; he slowed down until he saw the car. He did that not just to close the gap between them but to ensure that if there was a breakdown he knew it quickly because cell phone coverage was not available everywhere along the route to notify him of such a breakdown. The two teams arrived in Matotoka and parked in a convenient location away from fruit and meat sellers who normally came around cars displaying their wares. Both the teams had enough food and drinks and did not require anything from them. However they still came around. When they found them eating food prepared at home, they moved away quietly. The journey continued at a very slow pace across the potholes up to Makali, from where good road suddenly appeared before them, permitting a certain level of speed which enabled them to cover reasonable ground. Work was on going on the road, the reason for the sudden improvements which hid the potholes partially.

Sakayo and Kumba spoke in low tones to each other followed by smiles. They were not as comfortable in the company of Entona and Betty as they would have been if they were by themselves. They enjoyed being together and did not feel the trauma of the multiplicity of the potholes and the heavy gallops that they went through before they came to the better road.

The teams arrived at the Junction from where they followed the road to Kayima. They drove through many villages and towns and arrived in Kayima when there was still sun light.

The two cars moved across the town to the Chief's compound. Immediately a crowd started forming around the Chief and Entona and especially around Betty. The crowd grew until Entona received the keys to his house and Sakayo moved the car over there. Kaye followed them to help with the packing of the items into the house. But by the time he arrived there, the youths were already busy removing the items from the car to the house. The crowd moved from the Chief's house to Entona's house and watched every event. Sakayo and Kumba were quite busy packing the rooms. They got Entona's room ready and then the two other rooms, one for Kaye and wife and the other for themselves. Kumba Kaye was encouraged to stay with them at Entona's house until the next day. They settled down and the ladies served the cooked food from the cooler. They ate on time and were quite satisfied. After dinner they received many visitors who stayed around for a while and left early to allow them to rest properly. Some had come purposely to see what Betty looked like after many years of separation, and when they saw her they were amazed. She was round and well dressed in wax cotton with a beautiful hair style. Indeed she looked like somebody from the city. Some others came there to see whether Entona and Betty were truly reunited, and they saw with their own eyes the way they were close together and concluded for themselves that they were again husband and wife. Others still came out there to see how much goods she brought and that was not very difficult to prove as they saw each and every item that went from the car into the house. They concluded that she was indeed better off than most of them. Hawa was in the crowd with Mary and she led her into the house as soon as the visitors started to receive their own visitors inside. And after a joyful reunion with Mary, Betty gave her biscuits and some of the bread they bought in Freetown. From that moment she never allowed herself to be separated from Betty from that moment. The next day Sakayo and Kumba woke up very early because they went to bed early. As she was contemplating on breakfast and how to go about it without wood, there was a tap on the door. It was Fanta, the Chief's wife. She came in with two big bowls of cooked cassava and soup for breakfast. The bowls were hot and neatly covered with some thick napkin to keep them hot until the guests were ready for breakfast. She went back home and within a short time she came back with a plastic bucket of hot water for each person in turn and finally for Kumba Kaye. All guests had their bath and then Kumba served breakfast. They enjoyed cassava and groundnut soup very much and praised Fanta for a job well done.

Before the visitors started arriving, Sakayo prepared three envelopes with reasonable sums of money enclosed. He gave the first envelope to his parents for their resettlement. The Chief received the second envelope for his courageous intervention into the domestic financial affairs of his father towards Mary. The third envelope went to Hawa for her care and concern for Mary. Most of the day was spent in talking to the elderly, or to the young men of the town. Some of the young men were either Sakayo's and Kaye's classmates or school mates. It was a joyful reunion of people who once lived together long ago. In the afternoon Sakayo and Kaye, in the company of their wives, strolled the length and breadth of the town. At every strategic stop-over either Kaye or Sakayo explained particular events which concerned them when they were in School. In particular, Sakayo showed the group the trees which he climbed, including the mango tree from which he saved Suku's life. It was indeed a long walk around the town with a large following. Hand in hand with their wives, they walked side by side, attracting attention wherever they stopped to discuss. The teenage boys and girls in the group admired the couple so much that they wished they could be like them. Kaye and yei drove to Siwaya to meet her relatives, his in- laws. It was a short distance from Kayima and it took them a short time to arrive there. They found them waiting, as a message had been sent there already. It was a good first encounter where Kaye got to know most of his in- laws and they in turn got to know him. The couple gave to the head of the family a big brown envelope containing some money for the entire family. The family in turn gave to the couple some rice, cocoa yam, some beans and live chickens. Kaye and Kumba too spent some time with her aunt and other relatives and gave them some money in fulfillment of some of the requests they had made to him earlier. Before the evening Kaye and Yei returned to Kayima and joined Sakayo and Kumba. The couples had accomplished all that they had planned to do in the village, including seeing some authorities who may have played some important roles in their lives. They were happy but exhausted and were quite ready for the return trip the next morning. Over night they packed their luggage and stayed awake for most of the night. They got up early the next morning and left when most people were yet asleep. The first cock crow found them beyond the Sewa Bridge. Kaye and Yei led the way followed closely by Sakayo and Kumba. In both vehicles the couples discussed, argued but everything ended in laughter and smiles. The journey was convenient and they were in no haste to get back to Freetown. So they drove with ease and stopped anywhere they wanted to, especially to clear a point or to emphasis a point to each other. There were few vehicles on the high way that morning which also made the driving not too challenging. Sakayo overtook when he realized that Kaye was slowing down very often. But when he led the way he did worse. Nevertheless, Kaye was patient with him to lead until they arrived in Matotoka, where they stopped to shop. They climbed down the vehicles and bought some fresh fruits and some bundles of cassava. They were very careful not to touch anybody whilst they were in the market, and at the end of the shopping they sanitized their hands before moving on. They kept strictly to the rules of hand washing and avoided bush meat, at least temporarily. They were indeed happy and that made them forget to a large extent the Ebola, its doubtful origin and the devastating effect on the population. They sped behind each other across the towns to avoid any breakdowns in an area with suspected cases of the Ebola. When they were In Waterloo, they stopped to augment their fruits and cassava stock but the crowd was so large that they decided to abandon that plan and moved ahead without much delay. At Jui Junction they stopped and bought some cold drinks in the super market by the Gas Station. It was there Kaye refueled and decided to use the Regent Road, the newly constructed first class route to Freetown. But Sakayo and Kumba wanted to buy some items at a popular location known as PZ; so they used the highway to Freetown. Kaye and Yei were rather in haste to get back home quickly because Yei had her final examinations the following month. But before they took off he came around and spoke to Kumba passionately for the first time since she got married. He bid her farewell in a manner which symbolized a final break between them. He climbed the vehicle where Yei waited patiently, looked back at Kumba, waved and then moved on. "I am now completely yours. My brother has said a final goodbye to me" said Kumba smiling.

"This is how it should be. A man shall leave his father and mother and cleave onto his wife and the two shall be one," he said laughing. They finished their drinks and drove through Calaba town, Wellington, Kissy Road up to PZ and parked the vehicle along Garrison Street, the next street to PZ. They walked around to buy the few items they needed and returned to the vehicle within a short time to prevent thieves from breaking into it. He then drove along Siaka Stevens Street heading for Brookfields. "Watch out," Kumba shouted. Sakayo slowed down and saw a dog lying in a pool of blood, smashed by another vehicle. Kumba looked away as he drove past it. "This is the fate of many street dogs in the city. When you start driving you will encounter a lot of them on the high way," he said and touched her thick black hair that rested on her shoulders. "We have not discussed my job plans at any time. What are your plans?" she asked.

"I am looking at the newspapers but no relevant job has come up so far. I am quite convinced that very soon you will have something, being a highly qualified person. But don't you know that you already have a job, to take care of my baby for which I am prepared to put you on a good salary?," he said and there was laughter in the vehicle until they arrived home, parked the vehicle, and got the luggage and goods out into the house and store. Kumba prepared some bread with sardines and mayonnaise for dinner, with two cups of hot tea with lime. They took their dinner quickly, discussed briefly and went to bed as it was getting dark around them. In the bedroom it was all joy, jokes and laughter until both of them fell asleep.

Betty got news of her success in her nursing examinations and posting to Koidu Government Hospital barely a month after they returned to Kayima. It was good news everywhere at home; Entona back at work, Mary back home, and Betty with a new job. Mary received many gifts from Betty which she considered to be a show of love and she was happy to stay with her. Besides, she felt liberated from the excessive scrutiny and monitoring by her own mother. She understood quite clearly that what she was doing was in her own best interest and she took it seriously but Nema overstretched her to the point of cutting her off completely from boys. She was in Fasuluku Memorial Secondary School and she was quite aware of the issues and Nema's concerns but she was quite determined to overcome all the hindrances that would keep her out of school because Sakayo had promised to support her education fully.

She managed the home well when Betty took up her job as a nurse in the Koidu Government Hospital. But Betty made sure she was in Kayima most weekends to provide support to her in her school work and with the domestic work. Mary received assistance from Nema and once in a while she went to see her in Koidu town. On her first visit she explained to her that Betty was a nurse at the Koidu Hospital. She stopped what she was doing and stared at her for a long time. "Do you mean a nurse?"She asked. "Yes a nurse" She replied. "Well, I am always reminded of the illicit abortion that I did when I hear the word "nurse". If it was not by God's Grace I would not have had you as my only daughter because of the damage the nurse did on my womb during the illicit abortion" she explained. "Aunty Betty is not just an ordinary nurse, she studied at Connaught Hospital and passed her examinations which qualified her to be posted to Koidu town Hospital" She explained. "Praise the lord for her meaningful success. Please continue to obey her and do not ignore any pieces of advice from your father. And above all, don't break communication with Sakayo your brother. Whenever he is around let me know, there is a need to apologize to him" she started to confess then stopped. "Mama, apologize for what?" She queried. Nema stared at her and tears filled her eyes. "Apologize for being unkind, wicked and selfish to him. It is a long story my daughter but I am guilty. Please forgive me too for being unkind to your brother. I am now ashamed of myself because I know from all indications how much Betty loves you. God have mercy on me" She prayed with her hands raised above her head. Mary too could not hold back her tears when she heard her mother's confession and its implications for the family. She was embarrassed but she was quite convinced that she confessed from her heart which was the right thing to do.

Meaning of some unfamiliar words, terms and other clarifications:

Shebureh- Local musical instrument made of beads, thread, and buttons neatly fitted to a dried and processed special gourd with a long natural handle (a local tambouring).

The average exchange rate during the period of writing: $1=Le 7,400

Bondo Society- This is a powerful women's organization which is responsible for Female Genital Mutilation (FGM) of teenage girls. It has the support of some local chiefs and some politicians and it is practiced in all provincial cities, towns and villages and in most part of the capital city, Freetown.

Court Barray- A local court house/ building where justice is administered in the provinces of Sierra Leone.

www.ingramcontent.com/pod-product-compliance
Lightning Source LLC
Chambersburg PA
CBHW020954180626
46814CB00003B/1080